SERIES

SILVER

SERIES

**SUPERB WRITING
TO FIRE THE IMAGINATION**

Tanith Lee writes, 'When I write I go to live inside the book. By which I mean, mentally I can experience everything I'm writing about. I can see it, hear its sounds, feel its heat or rain. And its characters become better known to me than the closest family or friends. This makes the writing-down part very simple most of the time. I only need to describe what's already there in front of me. That said, it won't be a surprise if I add that the imagined worlds quickly become entangled with the so-called 'reality' of this one.'

'Since I write almost every day, and think (and dream) constantly about my work, it occurs to me I must spend more time in all those other places, than here.'

She began writing when she was nine and has not stopped since. With 15 children's books, 42 adult novels, almost 200 stories, four radio plays and two episodes of the cult television science fiction series *BLAKE'S SEVEN* to her name, she has won the World Fantasy Award twice and the August Derleth Award. This first story in the WOLF TOWER sequence was shortlisted for the Guardian Children's Fiction Prize.

Law of the
WOLF TOWER

Tanith Lee

*Hodder
Children's
Books*

a division of Hodder Headline

First published in Great Britain in 1998
by Hodder Children's Books
This Hodder Silver Series edition published 2000

A Catalogue record for this book is available
from the British Library

ISBN 0340 77828 8

Typeset by Palimpsest Book Production Limited
Polmont, Stirlingshire

Printed and bound in Great Britain by
Guernsey Press Co. Ltd, Channel Isles

Hodder Children's Books
A Division of Hodder Headline
338 Euston Road
London NW1 3BH

Break the rules.
Traditional

Contents

THIS BOOK

Yes.

I stole this. This book.

I don't know why. It looked – nice, I suppose, and nothing has been nice for years. Well, not often.

It was in her stationery chest, out of which, sometimes, she makes us – mostly me – get her a piece of silk-paper or thick parchment. Then she doodles a few stupid lines of *awful* 'poetry'. Or a foul painting, like used washing-water in the Maids' Hall with something dropped in it – lime-juice, or jam. And then we all have to applaud. 'Oh! How clever you are, Lady Jade Leaf. What bright-shining genius!' Because she's royal. And we are not. Oh no. We couldn't *ever* do anything wonderful like *that*.

Frankly, I think I could spit in a more interesting pattern. As for the poems—

Here is the latest example:

> *I drift like a petal all upon the air*
> *And the roses bow.*

Drift like a petal . . . She's more like a hippopotamus in the river. I don't mean fat – Lady Iris is fat, but she's also glamorous and graceful. Jade Leaf is slim. But the way she moves—

If the roses bowed they did it because they fainted with fright, screaming: 'Don't let that great thing bash into me!'

(Having said this, I feel I should add hippopotami are graceful, too, underwater.) (Besides, a hippopotamus has never picked up its little ornamental cane and cracked me across the palms of my hands so they bled. Which Jade Leaf has done so many times, I can't remember the number.)

If you found this, and are now reading it, need I ask you not to tell anyone? But hopefully you aren't. I'm just imagining you.

And there's someone banging for real on the door, which means I have to go and do something so much more important, that is, attend Jade Leaf.

I'll write my name here. After that, you'll know it's me.

Claidi.

Midnight. (I just heard the House clock.) Sky a sort of thick stirred-up black, milky with stars.

Vile day. Daisy broke a vase and Lady Jade slapped and slapped her, till Daisy cowered on the floor. Then Lady JL kicked Daisy with her silk slippered foot. Daisy has bruises, and is also

10

expected not to be given any dinner in the Maids' Hall for nine nights. Pattoo and I put some of our food in a napkin and gave it to Daisy when we went to bed. Pattoo and Daisy are sleeping now.

I'm so tired I have to stop too.

Absolutely nothing to write. It's seven days since the last thing I wrote. But nothing ever happens, here.

No, wrong. There was a dust storm yesterday that blew in from the Waste, and the slaves ran to work the fans, and pull up the slatted roofs over the best parts of the Garden. In the House all the windows and doors were shut and everybody was cooped up and bad-tempered.

LJL had a tantrum. She screamed and yelled and threw things. Then she was ill and had to lie down, and we put cloths soaked in cool scented water on her forehead. If it dripped in her eyes, she screamed again. We all had headaches, but no cool water-cloths for *us*.

I hate this place.

Nothing to write.

Except Pattoo and I were prevented by the Maids' steward from putting aside food for Daisy. She cried with frustration (and hunger) but now she's gone to sleep.

Perhaps I should say, we share this tiny room in the Maids' Hall, and have three narrow mattresses, and one mirror and one chest. These are not our possessions, you understand, but things *lent* to us, like our clothing, by Lady J and her mother, the Princess Shimra.

Sometimes we steal two or three flowers from the Garden and put them in a jar in the narrow window. But flowers don't last, do they.

Nothing to write.

NTW.

There seems no point, really, I sternly say to myself now, in having thieved this book, so craftily and unsensibly, if I'm not going to put anything in it.

Any news? Well, today was the Ritual of the Feeding of the Red Birds.

We went to the Red Aviary, a bird house full of feathers and trills and tweets. They fly about freely here, between the trees that grow up through the floor into the glass roof. They look, the birds, like flying flowers of crimson and scarlet, but the squeaks are sometimes piercingly loud, and also droppings fall on everyone, despite the parasols we dutifully hold over our ladies' heads.

The birds today are fed special grains and seeds, dyed matching or toning bird colours.

I like the birds a lot, but the smell is pretty overpowering.

Later there was an ordinary storm. Colossal bangs

of thunder as if gigantic trays were being dropped in the sky. Lady JL is loudly afraid of the thunder and the lightning, but I ran off and watched from an upper window. Next, summoned back to *her*, she said where had I been, told me where – she was wrong – then that I was a lazy slut, and predictably cracked me over the hand with her cane. Only one hand, though, the left one, so I can still write this.

Oh, and Daisy, who has been eating so much at dinner every night, making up for the nine missed ones, was violently sick all over the Maids' Hall floor, which had just been cleaned.

I ask myself, if you are reading this, (and haven't got bored with it all, as bored as I get with it all, and flung it on the rubbish dump or in a fire) I ask myself, what you might find interesting to have me tell you.

Because perhaps you don't live in the House or the Garden, but have somehow come from somewhere else. This seems unlikely, but then you aren't real, are you, just some wonderful intriguing imaginary person I've made up. My fantasy.

So, I'll pretend you're keen to know . . . Shall I? Or not.

I'm sort of an orphan. My parents aren't dead – although I suppose they might be, in fact, by now. That's a grim thought. But I can't even really feel much about it, because I never knew them.

There are so many Rituals. The House and the Garden live by them. What else is there to do? But the Rituals are taken entirely and stonily seriously. They're immovable. And if you profane a Ritual – if you break one of the idiotic rules of this place – you're punished.

Sometimes they're only slight mistakes and the punishments aren't too bad. (Let's say you miss lighting every single candle in the Lighting of the Candles Ritual, or do it in the wrong order. Then you might only have to stand in the Black Marble Corridor for a few hours, something like that – though your lady would probably beat you, too.) But for profaning some of the most important Rituals and rules, the punishments are fierce. The worst punishment, of course, is to be exiled to the Waste.

It's a death sentence. At best, if you *do* survive, a living nightmare. Hell-on-earth.

The Waste is the worst thing in the world.

This is what they tell you.

It is always stressed how grateful we should be, that we were born here, the House, the Garden, this earthly paradise, and not out there, in the Waste. I can recall them drumming this into me when I was a child, a baby, and crying for my mother and father. To be an orphan, and the maid of a (cruel) lady in paradise, was better than existing in the Waste.

The weather there is unthinkable. White hot heats, freezings, rains of *stones*, gales that tear up the dry

14

starving landscape. There are terrible mountains of black rock, and from there the dust storms come which sometimes pass over the Garden. In the Waste you go hungry always, and thirsty. Water is poisoned. Nothing grows, or if it does, it's horrible to look at and disgusting to eat.

No wonder the people and *things* that survive out there are peculiar and dangerous. Madmen, murderers and monsters roam.

From a couple of the highest towers of the House, if you're willing to climb hundreds and hundreds of stairs – I have – you can just glimpse something beyond the edges of the fortressed Garden walls. That must be the Waste. But you can't see much. Only a sort of threatening, shimmering vagueness. A pale *shadow*.

Once a lion got into the Garden. A monster lion from the Waste. This was in the year before I was born. It was an ugly and lethal beast, foaming flame, they say, from the mouth. So they killed it.

But why have I gone on so about all that, the outside world, which I've never even seen?

Because my parents profaned one of the greatest Rituals. (I don't know which one.) They were promptly exiled to the Waste.

Now I can't sleep. There are clusters of huge blistering blue-white stars.

Tomorrow is the Ritual of the Planting of the Two Thousandth Rose.

We have to be up extra early, before dawn.

I feel strangely guilty, since I think I'm going to stop writing in this book. Which makes me aware that I've mistreated it, the book, I mean, taking it and then spoiling it with my writing. And then worse, stopping.

But what is there to say? I'm sorry, if you've read this far. But then you haven't.

Something INCREDIBLE. Something unthought of and impossible – has occurred.

I have to organize my mind, which feels as if it's whirling about, and my heart is bird-flying and flapping around inside me. I keep laughing out loud.

I'm not in our room. I've climbed up to another place. I'm sitting here, but inside me everything is jumping and spinning. How can I start to tell you?

Let me go back, back to the morning, and begin again.

EXCITEMENT BY AIR

The Garden stretches for many miles in all directions, away from the House.

We walked slowly down the green, closely-cut lawns, Pattoo, Daisy and I. And then down lots of mossy steps, with mossy statues standing by them.

The Gardeners keep everything perfect, and the slaves attend to all the cunning mechanisms that keep the Garden watered and nourished. The Garden is even kept warm, when the weather turns cold, by a system of underground furnaces and hot-water pipes, quite like those used in the House.

Aside from maintenance, the Garden is also very artistic, to please the royalty. Here and there, areas may even look a little overgrown, or there might be a pavilion a bit ruined. But the overgrowings are always carefully clipped to just the right amount of wildness, and the ruin will be clean and gleaming, with ivy trained up on wires. Even decay is planned here, and controlled.

The House, which is the centre of the Garden, showed from the steps, every time we took a left turn. I'll describe it quickly. It's a terraced building, with columns, white and pink, and with sloping roofs scaled in dark green and gold.

Above, through the leaves, the sky was that breath-taking blue that sings. The sort of sky that makes you feel something astonishing and marvellous is about to happen – only it never does.

'Oh, come on, come on,' panted Pattoo. She's always nervous. She likes to please. Which is sensible really. She's seldom beaten.

But Daisy snapped, 'I can't go any faster. I've already spilled some of this filthy stuff. Do you think they'll notice?' She added to me.

'Umm.'

Perhaps they wouldn't. There are twenty or so Ritual oils that have to be brought to any special planting in the Garden, each of them highly scented and sticky.

Daisy's flagon of oil was noticeably low, and besides you could see the mark on her dress where most of it had gone.

(We were wearing melon green today, to tone with Jade Leaf's deeper green dress. And our hair was powdered *paler* green. The ladies generally insist their maids complement their own choice of colours. An order arrives before every function. The dresses too weren't comfortable. For the past month or so the fashion has been for stiff-bodied, ankle-length silk tubes, which is all right in a way if you're not big, though Pattoo is rather. But when it comes to walking, you have to take mincing little tiny steps, or you a) rip the dress, or b) fall over flat.)

Pattoo and I scrubbed Daisy's dress-tube with our decorative gauze scarves. This made things worse.

'Stand behind us,' I said. 'She may not see.'

But Jade Leaf almost certainly would.

We teetered on.

The sun was hot, but beautiful fragrances throbbed from the flowers. Sculpted woods and thickets poured down towards the river, which sparkled.

It's a lovely place, to be honest. I mean, it is to look at. And for royal people I'm sure it's lovely altogether.

At the bottom of the mossy steps, the lion house runs behind gilded bars. The lion house is large, complicated-looking, and their whole enclosure is enormous. But the House lions are normally on view. They seem to put themselves where they can be admired. They play and sleep and sun themselves, and are very peaceful. Sometimes they're even brought out on a jewelled lead, and royal ladies and gentlemen walk about with them, and feed them sweets.

The lions seem contented, like the House hippopotami, and all the other animals here. They never have to hunt or fight, everything's given them. They're even groomed by slaves. But every year there are less. They can't even be bothered to have families.

I used to wonder, when I was a child, if these creatures *missed* something? Of course they do.

Another terrace went down in steps of marble, and there were fountains, and pools with golden fish, and lilies.

Then, the Rose Walk.

The smell is astounding, it makes you dizzy. Roses rise on every side, in arches and tiers and cushiony banks. They're every shade of red and purple, yellow and white.

Wicked thorns like claws scratched at us as we wended through, and Daisy almost spilled the rest of her oil.

In the centre of the Rose Walk is a big oval of

grass, and a statue of a rose, carved out of some shiny stone.

This is where the Two Thousandth Rose was to be viewed before planting.

It was apparently a very startling and special rose. One is always bred by the Gardeners for this Ritual, which takes place every three years.

You may wonder how there was ever room for a new rose in this dense chaos of roses. But obviously other roses die, or are weeded out mercilessly when the princes and princesses get irritated with them.

Not that many of the royalty had come to the Ritual, (a lesser one). It was a hot day, even though the sun had been up less than an hour.

We went and took our stations behind Lady J. No maids are allowed to arrive until this moment, and others were coming in from all sides of the Rose Walk, but Lady J seemed to think we were late.

'Why are you always dawdling?' she snapped. We bowed our heads looking properly ashamed. Daisy edged in close behind me to hide the spill-stain. 'You're moronic,' decided LJL.

She has a pointy face, rouged all rosy, and now her hair was powdered a kind of cabbage colour.

Her mouth sneered over her sharp little teeth.

'You deserve a slap,' she said to me.

I lifted my head, and looked at her. She doesn't like that. But then she hates me anyway, even if she would never admit to hating something as low as a maid.

'Don't you stare at me,' she rasped. But I'd already bowed my head again. 'I'm so tired of you, Claidi. I can't even beat any sense into you. I've asked mummy, and she says she'll have you properly whipped, if you won't pull yourself together.'

Then her little eyes went over me and fixed on Daisy.

In all her green, Jade Leaf went the colour of an exploding raspberry. 'Why you ghastly little *beast*—' she shrieked, 'that gown – you've ruined it—'

Heads turned.

Princess Shimra spoke coolly nearby, in the cluster of ladies, 'Calmly, Jade Leaf. You'll give yourself another headache.'

Several princesses murmured soothingly, slinking and swaying like one more bed of lushly tinted plants.

JL lowered her voice and leaned towards us like a snake.

'*Expect* something,' she said. 'And you too, Pattoo. You'll have done something, even if I can't see it.'

I was already frightened. She'd never threatened me with a proper professional whipping from her mother's steward before. Now I went cold. Daisy was breathing fast, and Pattoo had crumpled. It was so unfair. *She'd* done nothing at all.

But now the Gardeners were pompously bringing the Two Thousandth Rose, in a gilded basket, and the royal ones were bending over it and exclaiming.

It reached Lady J, and she too peered down.

What a nasty sight. This green and puce monster craning in over the new rose, which was itself extremely hideous.

It was exactly the colour Daisy's sick had been. And it was a funny squirty shape. And it had a perfume which, even through all the other perfumes, was so *sweet* it could make you gag.

'Ah, how lovely,' swooned LJL, gentle and melting.

She undoubtedly thought it was.

Oh, I could have killed her. I truly would have liked to, right then and there.

We were all for it anyway. And why? I'd merely glanced up. Daisy had spilled the rotten oil because she had to wear a stupid fashion. Pattoo had simply been there.

My eyes burnt. No one was more suprised than me to see a huge burning tear-drop, heavy as a hard-boiled egg, thump, from each of my eyes. They plunged into the lawn.

As I was gawping at this extraordinary thing, everyone else began to shout and howl, and a hot and frantic sensation filled the rose-thick walk.

Like a fool, I thought they were angry at me for spilling *tears*.

Then I looked up again, and it wasn't me at all.

You can't always see the moon. At night, sometimes the clouds are thick as wool. And in the daylight, if the moon is there, it's transparent as a soap bubble.

Now I could see the moon clearly by day, and it was quite beautiful, and odd. It was a silver globe, shining bright, and slimly striped with soft red.

Something seemed to hang under it, an anchor perhaps, to moor it to the ground when it set?

Which was fanciful and silly, because the moon wasn't like that at all. And this was decidedly *not* the moon.

Princess Flara yowled, 'An invasion! An enemy! Help! Save us all!'

Panic.

I had seen this happen years ago, also in the Garden, when a swarm of bees suddenly erupted from a tree. Princes and princesses, ladies and gentlemen, and all their flounced and spangled kids, wailing and honking and running for their lives.

I'd been a kid myself, about six, and I just sat down on the grass and waited for the bees to go by. Usually if you leave them alone they don't sting you.

However, this was not a bee. What was it?

Someone supplied the answer, which also made no sense.

'A hot-air balloon – a *balloon*—!'

They were off anyway. Galloping up the lawn and on to the paths of the Rose Walk. I noted lots of tube dresses had already been split, some up to the waist! – and lots of sticky oil was being spilled.

I looked at Daisy and Pattoo. A few of the other maids, and a handful of slaves were lingering too, scared but undecided.

The 'balloon' passed over the upper air, and was hidden behind a stand of large trees.

Pattoo said, 'We ought to follow Lady Jade.'

'Bees to Lady Jade,' I muttered, nostalgically.

Daisy blinked. 'But if it's an *invasion*—'

Invasion, by the Waste. Where else could it come from?

Another of the maids, dressed in tasteful parchment silk, said uneasily, 'Once a madman from the Waste flew over in a – *balloon* – and poured burning coals on the Garden!'

'When was that?' Daisy, wide-eyed.

'Oh . . . once.'

The slaves were trotting off into the trees. A slave hasn't ever much time for him-or-herself, so even the moments before we were invaded or had burning coals slung at us, were valuable.

Pattoo though turned resolutely and began to pad heavily up the path after LJL, who had promised us all 'something' bad.

Daisy reluctantly said, 'We'd better.'

The others were also drifting off, upset and dutiful together.

If I stayed here, unless the invasion was total and

nothing mattered any more, then I'd be blamed, and I was in trouble already.

Just then we heard the alarm trumpets and bells sounding from the House.

We ran.

Earlier, I think I said I wondered what you might find interesting, but I didn't tell you much, did I? I apologize.

I didn't, for instance, tell you about the House Guards.

Didn't want to, probably.

As we came up on the higher lawns, with our ridiculous tube skirts clutched up to our knees (most unruly) to stop them tearing, the Guards were swarming through the Garden.

Sometimes you don't see them for days. Unless your lady sends you into a part of the House, on an errand, where they are. LJ seldom did.

When I was little, I was horribly frightened of the Guards. I believe some really nice clever person had told me I'd better behave, or the House Guards would 'get me'.

They're there to defend us. Royalty first, naturally. But also the lowest of the low like servants, maids and slaves. They guard places in the House, too, the Debating Hall, for example, and the upper storeys where the royalty sleep. But they are mostly in their own guard tower, which is one of the highest towers of the House, even taller than the ones I spoke of with hundreds of steps.

The Guards wear blackest black, crossed with belts of silver, and slashed with epaulets of gold. They have high boots shiny as black mirror, with spikes sticking from the heel and the toe. They have knives in fancy scabbards, rifles decorated with silver, and embroidered pouches to carry shot. Medals cover them like armour.

Now they had on their copper helmets too, which have vizors, and more spikes pointing up from the top.

They looked like deadly beetles.

We cowered back among a fringe of rhododendrons, but one of the Guards turned and bellowed at us in a sort of hating voice:

'Get inside, you damned rubbish!'

Daisy caught her breath, and I heard another maid start to cry. But everyone was scared already. And we bolted on for the House up the terraces and steps.

The Guards were dragging black cannon on black gun-carriages.

I saw a maid – Flamingo, I think – accidentally get in their way, and one of the Guards thrust her aside, so viciously, she sprawled.

In order to protect us properly, they were quite prepared to do us harm. In fact they seemed eager to hurt us, perhaps a sort of practice.

I ducked under a buckled, black-clad arm. Pattoo

was dragging. I caught at her and hauled her with me.

And there was the House, sugary and cute in sunlight.

The *balloon* seemed to have vanished.

Had we all dreamed it?

No, for the Guards were angling every cannon one way. I could smell gun-powder.

I'd heard of events like this, but never seen – smelled – one.

Just then, over a crest of poplar trees, the balloon drifted back again into sight, like a charming toy.

The Guards roared. They appeared to have forgotten us.

It seemed crazy to be out in the open, but somehow we stood and gaped up at the silvery bubble I'd mistaken for the moon.

And in the crystal windows of the House, there was face upon face, (like piled vegetables) pink, tawny, black, all the royal ones, glaring up into the sky, having pushed such unimportant beings as *maids* out of the way.

I grabbed Pattoo again. 'Look.'

'I don't want to,' she said, and she hid her eyes. Daisy was too scared to look away.

And I – I couldn't either.

Then there was a sizzling sound, and the cannons blasted, one, two, three, four of them. The noise – there were clouds of stinking smoke and bits of fire splashed all around.

(Tinder has almost an almond smell, I absurdly thought, like marzipan for a cake . . .)

The balloon turned over, a wonderful fruit disturbed up on the tree of the sky.

Even like that, it looked effective. But then there was another burst of flame, up where the balloon was. And it reeled sideways. And then it began to fall. It looked so soft, as if there was nothing to it – the stuff you blow off a dandelion.

But when it dropped behind the trees, there came a terrific thud. The ground shook. Smoke bloomed up there like a new plant.

It was only then the House Guards gave a raucous cheer. They were yelling, as if in a game, 'A *hit*!' And 'Well done, Jovis.' And 'Think we killed him?'

HIM

When we got into the House, everyone was going mad. People were running along the corridors, colliding when two or more were coming from different directions. They were running up and down the stairs too, and sometimes tripping and falling. The row was almost as bad as the cannon.

Pattoo, Daisy and I ran up the stairs towards the apartments of our evil mistress.

When we reached the double doors, they were

open, and inside everyone also rushed about. JL sat in the middle of it all, screaming and pulling her own hair and thumping her fists on the sofa, and kicking her feet, off which her green silk shoes had flown.

She seemed worse than usual. I thought it was fear of the 'invasion', but surely she'd seen the balloon shot down?

Dengwi sidled up to me and hissed, 'She says insects have got into her dress. Fleas or bees or something.'

This nearly made me laugh. I'd wished bees on Jade Leaf, hadn't I.

I could see now the others were trying to get her dress undone, so they could sort out the situation, but LJL was in such a state they could hardly get near her. Suddenly she sprang up and ripped the dress in two bits with her own hands. She's strong. (All those smacks and beatings she's given have undoubtedly built up her wrists.)

There she stood in her lace-trimmed petticoat, snarling and pulling at herself.

The other maids began wiping and dusting her off. A few poor little ants were being murdered for daring to get into her gown.

I rushed forward too and began, more carefully, dusting the ants off, then carried the rescued ones and tipped them out of the window.

Outside, smoke still billowed over the Garden. Some of the Guards were marching up the Cedar

Walk, and there was someone, not a Guard, having to march in the middle of them.

'Is that — the *invader*?' whispered Daisy, letting go more ants to freedom down the wall.

'Must be.'

We tried to lean over and see more, but JL was screaming again even louder.

Daisy and I helped shake out JL's petticoat. Jade Leaf thrust us off, managing to poke Daisy in the eye.

'Oh you *filthyword* little sluts!' squawked JL.

Outside, they'd be marching right under the window now.

I leapt away and dashed back to the window, and looked down, calling as I did so, 'Oh, madam, the Guards have a prisoner.'

'Of course they have, you *extrafilthyword* little pest. Leave that, and come here. I'm covered in these *filthyword-Claidi-doesn't-even-know* things!'

Under the window, the ghastly Guards swaggering, and this man, sort of swaggering too. He wore a longish grey quite-military-looking coat, and the sun was gold, pure utter gold, all over his long, rough-cut hair. It didn't look possible, this hair. Powdered, perhaps? Didn't seem to be. It looked . . . *real*, in a way reality seldom manages.

Just then JL threw something at me — it was a paper-weight, I saw later — and it caught me sharp and cold with pain in my back. My breath went in a silly *oof*, and below, the prisoner, the invader, turned up his head to see, in the midst of capture, what creature it was that made such idiotic noises.

'Come here you filthy *filthyword*!' screeched dear Lady J.

I don't know what happened. I can't explain. Perhaps you can, perhaps it may, or something similar, have happened to you sometime.

Spinning round, I pelted straight at Jade Leaf. And as I reached her, I slapped her a huge stinging slap across half her disgusting pointy pink face.

Although the House was bursting with noise, this one room became completely silent. As if we had all been turned to stone.

I gazed at Jade Leaf, and had the thrilling joy of seeing the place I'd slapped turn from pink to boiling magenta.

Her mouth was wide open.

'You . . . hit me.'

'Lady,' I cried, very concerned, 'I had to. There was this awful insect on your cheek – you hadn't noticed. It might have stung you.'

But Jade Leaf only plumped down on the rug abruptly, like a child, and said, 'Hit me.'

'Yes,' said Pattoo, surprising me by her invention, 'look, madam.' And she showed JL a piece of squished fruit Pattoo must have got hold of just that moment to help me. 'It's horrible.'

'A good thing,' said Dengwi, 'Claidi acted so quickly.'

Jade Leaf's mouth opened more and her eyes were screwed away. 'Mummy!' she warbled. 'I want mummy!'

Magically on this cue, through the open doors stepped Princess Shimra in a cloud of attendants.

'Get up, Jade Leaf. What are you thinking of? The enemy balloonist has been taken to the Debating Hall. Change your clothes at once. Everyone will be there. Even Princess Jizania Tiger,' added Shimra, with wondering scorn.

To go to the Debating Hall everyone has to wear blue. I don't know why. It's yet another rule of the House.

Changing that hurriedly wasn't easy, although JL was abnormally docile.

We powdered her hair on top of the green and it looked fairly awful. Pattoo powdered the red slap-side of JL's face with white. Shimra hadn't even noticed.

We didn't have time for our own hair so we had to tie it in hasty untidy blue turbans.

My hands were shaking anyway.

The Debating Hall is huge, a high ceiling decorated with silver medallions, upheld by marble pillars, and below, a slippery polished floor. I know about the floor, because when I was nine or ten, I used to be one of the kids who polished it once every five days. And it took all day to do.

The ladies and princesses sat on their blue plush seats on the raised area, and the maids and servants and slaves gathered round to fan them and offer little tobacco pipes and calming drinks.

On the other side were the lords and princes, who, almost alone, make a decision at the end of every debate. However, at the head of the room was a long draped table, and behind that seven gilded chairs under a canopy. These are for the Old Ladies, the most ancient princesses. They too have an important vote.

Only three of the OL chairs were filled. There was Princess Corris, who's eighty, and Princess Armingat, who's eighty-five. They attend every debate, and argue wildly at the end, always disagreeing with each other.

Today a third chair had been filled.

Princess Jizania Tiger is said to be one hundred and thirty years old. She *does* look it. But she's absolutely beautiful. She seems made of the thinnest, finest pale paper. And her large hooded eyes are like pale amber pearls. She's bald, and wore today a headdress that was a net of almost colourless silvery beads, set occasionally with a bud of emerald. (She alone hadn't bothered with blue. Her gown was ash-coloured.)

I can't imagine ever being old, let alone old like this. But if I had to be, she would be my model.

She has a fine voice, too. Soft and smoky, musical. She only sounds about sixty.

As a rule though, she never bothers with debates. Only the most unavoidable dinners and Rituals.

It must be nice to get out of so many boring and unimportant things.

Now she sat there, leaning her slender old face on her slender crooked graceful hand, that had one colossal topaz burning on it in a ring.

The big space at the Hall's centre was fenced on two sides by weapon–bristling Guards, standing three deep.

I'd looked for him – I mean the prisoner, the enemy–invader – the moment we'd arrived. But the Guards are often dramatic. Only now did they march him in.

He seemed quite good–humoured, and certainly not upset. I wondered if he'd been hurt when the balloon fell, and was bravely hiding it.

The Guards left him alone in the middle of the Hall, and we all now glared down at him, and some of the royalty held up magnifying glasses.

Under the lighted lamps which are always lit in the hall, his hair looked like golden flames itself. The dark grey coat was swinging loose. He wore white under it, and boots that were a darker white. But mainly, he was young. Older than me, (did I say I'm about halfway through sixteen?) Eighteen maybe, nineteen. In what some of them call my Age–Group.

Despite that, the thing which is making this so hard to describe is that he had a gleam to him, a polish to him. I used to polish this floor, but *life* had polished this man. *Being* alive. *Living*. And he glowed.

He came from the unknown outside places, the Hell known as the Waste.

And I'd never thought anything that came from there could look any good. Terrifying, yes, revolting, probably. But not glowing and handsome, packed with energy, and this kind of easy pridefulness. With hair like melted sun.

One of the princes – Shawb – had risen, and now walked along the raised part of the hall, where the royalty were all sitting, until he came to the area just before the Old Ladies' chairs. Shawb turned swiftly and nodded to them. (Armingat cackled. Corris looked hungry for trouble. Jizania was unreadable.)

Then Shawb stared down long and hard at the prisoner.

'You speak, I understand, the language of the House.'

The prisoner shrugged slightly. 'Among others.'

'That doesn't interest me.'

'Nor me, really,' replied the prisoner.

I liked his voice. It was clear, and had a faint accent of something or other. I liked his cheek, too.

Shawb didn't.

'This isn't a joke. You're in a bad situation. Didn't you realize?'

'Well, after your men fired on me, and brought my craft down, I had an idea or two about it.'

The Guards growled. Shawb scowled.

'Your name?'

The prisoner half turned. He put a hand in a pocket of his coat, and at once a hundred knives and rifles were scraping up at menacing angles. But out of the pocket he only took a clean white handkerchief, very laundered.

'Nemian,' he said. 'That's my name.' And then he walked straight across the space they'd stood him in, right up to the (unguarded) table and chairs of the Old Ladies. He laid the handkerchief in front of Jizania Tiger.

During this Shawb was shouting and the lined-up Guards breaking ranks and I heard the rifles clicking and clacking, getting ready to fire. I'd dropped the fan I'd been supposed to wave, and put both my fists over my mouth. What a hopeless gesture. But I didn't know I'd done it until afterwards.

It was Jizania Tiger who held up her topazed hand.

'All right. What do you want, young man?' she asked in her excellent voice.

'To give you this, madam.'

'What is it? The rag you wipe your nose on?'

Nemian laughed. I liked his laugh. So did she. A carved little smile moved her lips.

'Of course it isn't, madam. It's a flower from the Waste. You might care for it.'

Shawb bawled, 'Don't touch the muck – it may be poisonous.'

But Jizania said, 'Not everything in the Waste is bad.'

I'd never heard anyone say *that* before. (It was then I noticed my fists clamped over my mouth and took them down.)

She'd unwrapped the handkerchief, and lifted up the flower. It really was one. It was fresh and firm, with big juicy green leaves, and the colour of the flower-head was crimson.

'Oh, yes,' said Jizania. As if she knew these flowers, although I'd swear there are none in the Garden, and so it *must* have come from the Waste.

And the Waste was Hell-on-Earth. So everyone had always said.

Nemian turned from Jizania with a bow. He looked round at all of us. He was smiling and unfussed, even though I now saw there was a streak of blood across his forehead. His eyes looked tired. I felt sorry about his eyes. I liked their colour, but I couldn't remember what it was. Only the shape, and the shadow.

He said, 'I'm on a search, a quest for something. I might have liked to visit your wonderful gardens, but alternatively I could just have gone elsewhere, if you'd preferred. In the end, I didn't have much choice, did I? You shot me down. I assume you're not used to visitors. Shame, really.'

Then he *yawned*.

I never saw anyone sit down so elegantly on a floor. Even when he was lying full length, he lay in a stylish way. Presently he seemed asleep.

Maybe you're getting used to my odd type of thinking. But I thought just then, all those days and months I'd polished the floor, and never knew one day he'd stretch out on it and lie there. There was a strange ache in my chest like the pressure of tears.

But the Guards milled forward now and surrounded Nemian so none of us could see him. It seemed they thought that by going to sleep, he'd performed another dangerous and life-threatening trick.

A few minutes after that, the Guards hustled almost all of us out of the Debating Hall. Only the most senior of the princes remained, Shawb among them. Even the Old Ladies were politely and firmly requested to go.

Jizania made no protest. The other two cackled and squeaked and struggled like nasty old children kicked out of a party.

In the outside chambers, the thrown-out royalty stood around chattering to each other. I thought Jade Leaf might be her usual self, but instead she went barging over to her mother, Princess Shimra.

'Mummy-mummy, can I stay with you?'

'I'm going to the library soon,' replied Shimra,

'to *read*,' looking uncomfortable as JL laid her head on Shimra's shoulder.

'Let me come too, mummy. I *want* to, mummy.'

'But you don't like reading, dear.'

Jade Leaf is about a head taller than Shimra, and now JL was acting like a little ickle girl, making her voice all gooey. This didn't happen often, thank goodness, as it makes you sick. Shimra as well, from the look of it.

Soon after that, Jizania Tiger swept by, her two attendants proudly holding up her long brocade train. When she had passed, Shimra had somehow escaped her daughter, and JL came disconsolately back to us, her maids. Her one-side-reddened face was cooler, but she still seemed to be confused. Had *I* done that?

But I didn't concentrate. I kept thinking of *him*.

What would they do to him? I'd only heard tales of punishments delivered to trespassers. Remember the lion, the one they killed?

We couldn't hang about though, for JL went off upstairs to the Jewellery Chamber, and we all had to go too.

When I was a child I liked this room, which has all the most ancient jewels and ornaments of the House displaid behind glass. Now that room only made me annoyed. I don't know why.

Today I barely saw it. Daisy seemed to be in the same state, and a couple of the others. Dengwi and Pattoo not.

I had an embarrassing idea Daisy and I at least had got a *thing* about Nemian. Yes, I had, I was sure. My face had gone hot simply thinking of his name.

This was dismal, wasn't it. I'd fallen for an outcast from Hell, who anyway they were going to kill. Besides which, he would never have glanced my pathetic way.

JL mooned over the bracelets and earrings. But gradually I could see the vagueness leaving her. The ickle girlie business. She had that snake-like air again. Not that I've anything against snakes – only the human ones.

'Claidi,' she said suddenly, very brisk and clear.

'Yes, lady?' I asked, my heart sinking even further. (Even with Nemian's arrival to distract me, I hadn't quite forgotten the professional beating.)

'Thank you so much for viciously slapping my face and destroying that dreadful insect. It was an insect, was it?' I attempted to seem bashful and pleased. 'I never knew you were so loyal. I ought to reward you.' She smiled brilliantly. 'When I tell mummy tonight, I'm sure she'll command her steward's whip-master to tie an extra-pretty ribbon on the whip. Do you know about the whip, by the way?' She bent closer. It didn't seem to be happening really. But a glass case pushed at my back and reminded me of where the paperweight she threw had bruised me. 'It's got spikes on it,' said LJL, triumphant. Ah, the whip had spikes.

She turned in her clumsy bulking way, and

knocked a case, which shuddered. As I was shuddering.

The other girls looked glum. But some ladies had come tinkle-rustling in, loudly exclaiming that the enemy-invader had been imprisoned in the Black Marble Pavilion.

Daisy gasped. Then I did, because one of the ladies turned to me and snapped, 'You, girl – Claidi-is-it?' 'Yes, madam.' 'Her Oldness, Jizania Tiger, wants you.'

Somehow I swallowed nothing the wrong way and choked. Pattoo thumped me on the back, luckily just clear of the bruise.

Dengwi guided me to the doorway. 'Listen,' she said, 'I don't know what the Old Lady wants, but everyone says she's all right. Appeal to her mercy. You *mustn't* be *whipped*. You do know, don't you, Claidi? My sister was, and—' Dengwi's face was like smooth black steel, 'she nearly died.'

I didn't know what to say. (Had I ever heard Dengwi had a sister?) There wasn't time anyway. A slave of the Old Lady's was standing there, looking haughty and patient, because a slave of an Old Lady had more status than anyone's maid.

My head was already whirling inside. So much was happening in my life where, as you know, for sixteen-ish years, nothing had happened at all.

The Lion in the Cage

I'm staring up at the moon, which, ironically, is visible tonight. Again ironically, I keep hearing a piece of LJL's terrible poetry: *O moon, of liquid floating lemon-green—*

In a way I feel sorry for her now. That's no doubt pretty stupid of me. But she's so hopeless. I mean, there really isn't a shred of hope for her. She'll always be like that, mean and spiteful and unjust and downright appalling. She isn't happy. If she were happy she'd be different. Look at Lady Iris and Prince Eagle, and there are others. They're kind to their servants.

There's some lecture we were given, about the time I was polishing the floor where Nemian lay down so wonderfully and went to sleep. The lecturer told us hard work and suffering would fine our characters, make us *better*.

What a load of poo.

Anyway, here, at this very high up window, staring at the moon, the whirling in me and all of me trembling, and yet somehow *serene* – I can't be angry at Jade Leaf.

But I feel weird about the other maids, especially Daisy and Pattoo. Because I won't be able to say good-bye.

To get back to my story:
Jizania Tiger's haughty slave took me along the

glassy corridors (windows, burnished wood) and up marble stairs. We reached Her Apartment, and I found it was built up on a flat roof. There was a roof garden, with trees in pots, and a pool with a fountain and coloured fish.

The Old Lady was sitting in a room open to this garden.

She'd taken off her jewelled headdress, and I admired her well-shaped bald head. She truly is magnificent-looking. (But of course I have extra reasons to be impressed with her.)

'Sit down,' she said to me. 'Are you hungry? Thirsty?'

Startled, I mumbled I wasn't. Although my mouth was dry.

She seemed to know this, I suppose not too difficult. She had the slave pour me a glass of fruit juice, orange, I think, which we only ever had watered-down in the Maids' Hall.

'You have no notion,' she said, 'why you're here.'

'No, lady.'

'It's been a busy day so far,' she said. She gave a short bark of laughter, like one of the Garden foxes. Then she said, 'Jade Leaf is an unpleasant girl to serve, I should think. I intend to look into that. And no, I understand you can't agree. But your life, Claidi, won't have been much fun. Is that true?'

Amazing she knew my name. Amazing she'd singled me out.

I said, awkwardly, 'Well, not really.' I thought of Dengwi's words, and blurted, not having meant to so soon, 'I slapped Lady Jade Leaf's face today. And she says I'm to be properly whipped. The whip with — spikes.'

Jizania Tiger slowly raised her exquisite eyebrows.

'A slap? A whip with spikes? I don't recall such a whip. I think there isn't one.'

I was afraid for a moment. Dengwi knew there was.

Then Jizania added, 'However, just in case, perhaps we had better think of an alternative to the whipping.'

I blurted again 'Thank you, thank you'. I knew well enough Jizania had power in the House. If she promised it, I'd be safe. At least for now, which always seems all you can ever hope for.

A crazy thought came to me. Perhaps Jizania Tiger would make me one of her own maids. They were of a rarer breed than us, they didn't even use the Maids' Hall, but had their own rooms in the Old Lady's apartment.

Why such an extreme of good luck should come my way I couldn't imagine. This kept me cautious.

Then she said, without warning, 'And what did you think of the enemy-invader, the young man called Nemian?'

Did I go red? Somehow not. I think I was too surprised.

'Er – well – he er – well he's – er—' cleverly said I.

'A very awful enemy, wasn't he,' said Jizania. 'I'm sure you were terrified.'

It seemed daft to lie. Her eyes seemed to say she could read one's mind.

'He looked just like the princes here,' I said. 'Well, actually, better.'

'Yes,' she said, 'very fit and bold. And that hair.' She sounded younger than ever when she said this, only about fifty. I blushed after all. She took no apparent notice. 'And the flower he brought from the Waste. That was a shock, wasn't it, Claidi? Did you ever guess things might grow there, beautiful healthy things?'

'No, madam. I thought the Waste was all poisoned.'

'Some of it. Some.'

There was a gap then. My eyes roamed uneasily. She had a spectacular indigo-feathered bird on a perch, which sat looking at me with wise old eyes like hers.

All at once, Jizania Tiger rose, with a stiff old grace.

'Come along,' she said, as I scrambled up. Naturally I didn't impertinently ask where we were going.

Where we went however was through the room and a door, and down a back stair, a winding cranky stair with only the narrowest windows. Several floors must have gone by, and then she took a key from a bracelet, and unlocked a narrow door.

Outside the door was a hanging. Brushing that aside, we were in the Black Marble Corridor.

It's not a lovely place. They send you there at night for lesser punishment. Strange eerie sounds come through holes cunningly cut in the walls, and there are dim-lit dismaying pictures of executions and people being cast out into the Waste, crying and pleading not to be. I'd sat here on the floor as a kid more than once, and had nightmares afterwards, as they know you will.

At the end of the long corridor is a courtyard, and in that, the Black Marble Pavilion.

Another key from the bracelet opened the door to the yard.

Huge paved slabs sloped away to the Pavilion. Its black columns hold up a black cupola. Between the columns run black thick bars.

Above, the sun was shining, but the Pavilion looked like total darkness. I couldn't see through the bars and columns to anything.

But Jizania Tiger, with only me to attend her, went sailing out on the paving.

Immediately two House Guards came striding around the Pavilion.

They saluted and stood to attention for the Old Lady, but as she got near, one shouted:

'Wait, please, madam. The enemy prisoner is here.'

46

She just gave a nod.

'Why else am *I* here?'

'It's this, madam. The prisoner is an alien from the Waste. It would be better if you—'

'Tottered back to my easy-chair?' Her voice sliced him in two. He lost his stern military stance. 'Don't presume, my lad,' said Princess Jizania Tiger, 'to give orders to an Old Lady of the House.'

Now there was creepy-crawl rather than salute. 'Excuse me, madam.' (The other Guard was grinning.)

She swept on, and I with her.

Nemian was around the other side in the Pavilion-cage, where the Guards had been. Maybe they'd been insulting him, or just talking. Surely someone must be interested in the Waste just a teeny bit.

He stood there inside the bars. His coat hung over a bench. He looked – overpowering, so close. So I couldn't even squint at him.

'Oh,' he said. 'Hallo, madam. A great lady, and a girl in a blue dress with green hair tangling from a blue scarf.'

I could *feel* him staring at me, a long, long gaze. He, who would never have glanced my way.

'She is Claidi,' said Jizania Tiger. And next she said, 'Claidi for short, that is. Her full name is Claidissa Star.'

My head shot up. I goggled at her. Most unbecoming I must have appeared. I had no words. I'd even forgotten the gorgeous Nemian.

Was that — *that* — my proper name?

My arm aches from writing so much. But I can't stop. There isn't time. The moon's moved. Can I squeeze the rest in before I have to go down?

For a minute, dazzled by the new name, I didn't take in what the princess and the prisoner were saying to each other. They were talking about something.

I sort of came back to hear him say, 'It's kind of you to inquire, madam. I wasn't seriously injured, no. A handful of bruises, a scratch or two. The balloon brushed against some of your trees in falling, and I was able to swing out on a handy bough. Then the balloon veered again and crashed at quite a distance. I was damned lucky.'

'Lucky but damned?' said she.

Nemian smiled, and I saw him colour very slightly. My heart turned a somersault. I'd certainly remembered him again.

'Pardon my rough language, lady,' he said. 'I've been travelling some while, and lost my good manners.'

Then his eyes came back to me. For a moment they held mine and I seemed to be sinking in them. (Still can't recall their shade — blue — grey ???) (Soon I'll know.) Then he smiled such a smile. And I thought, I really am not going to be so totally, tiresomely *soppy*. So I frowned at him in a grave

48

and ugly way. And he laughed. And I turned my head. (Childish. I'd run out of ideas on coping.)

Nemian said to the princess, 'She seems to have had enough, Lady Claidissa Star.'

'I expect she wants her tea.'

'Then please lose no further time in seeing she gets it.'

I found she was turning me with her slender claws, and we were going back over the paving, the Guards saluting, and I was convinced I'd messed everything up. Whatever everything was.

Back in her apartment a carved table had been laid with the most delightful 'tea'. (Really it was lunchtime.) I thought she meant me to wait on her, but she said I was to sit down and eat the tea with her.

In fact she only drank a glass of iced chocolate.

(It would be madness not to note down at least some of the 'tea'. There were sliced peaches, and strawberries, in painted dishes, and cakes still hot, and biscuits in the shapes of birds, and white butter shaped like a rabbit. There were hot and cold drinks of all types. How the cups and glasses sparkled.)

What a shame I couldn't eat anything. I tried. I'd never been offered such a feast. But you'll grasp why I couldn't.

And when Jizania Tiger saw I couldn't, she started to talk to me, and what she said made it impossible for me to eat and drink even the crumbs and drips I'd been trying to get down my throat.

'So much is said,' she said, 'about the House. Long ago, the House was a sanctuary. It was a pleasant enough place. But now it's like an overwound clock. It goes in fits and starts and tells the wrong time.'

Then she said, 'They talk about the Waste too, and terrorize little children with stories of it. But you saw the flower. The Waste isn't as bad as it's made out, just as the House isn't as good.'

Then: 'That young man, our handsome prisoner. They don't know what to do about him. He meant us no harm, but they're so used, by now, to distrusting and fearing anything from outside, that they can only lock him away. They may keep him in that cage for years. Or, in some sudden unreasonable alarm, they may decide after all to murder him. Really, I think he should be allowed to escape, don't you? But then. Someone needs to assist him. I have the means, but I'm old. I can't be bothered with such an adventure.'

After this she looked into my eyes with her amber hawk's stare.

'Then there is you. You've had a deathly life here, Claidi, and what can you hope for or ever look forward to? Beatings, nastiness, endless uninteresting work. Perhaps a marriage with some suitably obedient servant, if even that's allowed. You too, my girl, ought to be let out of your cage.'

I hadn't followed it all, not properly. My heart followed though, in rattling leaps.

Was she saying what my heart thought she was?

'You see, Claidi, you're reckless enough, and young enough, and *bothered* enough. If I gave you the means to let Nemian out of the Pavilion, and spirit him away from the House and the Garden, and into the hellish Waste . . . which is the world . . . Would you?'

Yes, heart, you were spot on.

She said, 'The Waste is more than we know. And you've said yourself Nemian is a lord. He comes from somewhere just as grand, grander, no doubt, than here. And he would take care of you.'

Before I could think it through, I cried, 'Why would he? I'm only—'

'Only what? Only a lady's maid?'

I withered at her words. The truth of them made them less swallowable even than the food. Maid – I was a *slave*.

Princess Jizania Tiger half turned, and held out her wrist for the indigo bird to soar down to, weightless as muslin. As it perched there, she fed it peaches, which it tucked daintily into its beak.

'Claidi,' said Jizania Tiger, 'you recall that your parents were driven out in the first year of your life?'

'Y – yes.'

'They profaned a Ritual. A most serious one.'

'Yes.'

'You don't know what it was. No one has told you.'

I shook my head. The bird scanned me, and shook its head too, copying.

But then Jizania Tiger told me that the first profanation had been that my mother was a princess of the House, and my father her steward, and that the second profanation was *me* – the fact that I was born, because no one is allowed to be born here, save when permission has been granted, and *never* of mixed rank.

'They saw fit not to exile an innocent baby,' said Jizania Tiger. 'Instead they condemned you to a life of harsh service to the House. And Shimra, who was your mother's friend – a false one, evidently – gave you to her atrocious daughter, a human boil, that someone should burst. These things I saw, but I've said, haven't I, how old and lazy I am. Besides, until now there's been no way out. I must add, Nemian knows, since I've told him, you are royal.'

'Did he believe you?' I croaked.

'Do you?'

Do I? I don't know.

All I know is, she gave me every key I shall need to free him, (she has, she said, a key to each lock of the House and Garden.) And she's told me how to do everything, and where to go, and that it's my choice, all this. That I needn't. But then, the Waste has flowers in it, and Nemian's own house, whatever that is, is there, and also my parents, just possibly, somewhere, if they survived. My courageous parents who fell in love and dared let their love make *me*.

It's all tumbling through me. Not just love – I feel I'm made of racing water and drums, and fired up by lightning.

And you'll have known all the time that I'll do it. I'll free him, and go with him. Take the risk. Out *there* – Wouldn't you?

THE ESCAPE

By moonlight, the Garden looked heavenly – I mean like heaven, whatever that is, we never had it properly explained. But obviously, a lovely and special place. I felt a moment of terror. This was what I knew, good or bad.

She'd said I was reckless. I didn't feel it, just then. I wanted to creep back to the room in the Maids' Hall, and say Jizania had only just sent me away. Dengwi and Pattoo had the night duty with Jade Leaf, so even *she* couldn't complain. She couldn't anyway. The Old Ladies were so powerful.

Jizania had told me she would say she had kept me in her apartment to serve tea – she only ever had 'teas' never breakfasts or dinners. Then she'd dozed off – 'Naturally, old women always doze off,' said Jizania with a tiger's smile. I had then stolen all the keys and run away.

She would have to say that. They would think her careless and a fool, but clear of the crime of setting Nemian free.

She had added though, that next day, tomorrow, if there was no uproar — that is, if he hadn't escaped because I hadn't let him out — she would say nothing at all.

But I could picture what she'd think of me, Claidi the cowardly spineless creep.

Looking back on this now, I mean now it's too late, since I *did* do it and there's no going back, my nerves seem pointless.

Let me describe how the Garden looked though. I want to put it down, because I'll never see it again, will I. And the joke is, it *was* partly mine. If what Jizania said about my mother was true.

The trees rested like soft dark blue clouds, and tapering pale dark towers, asleep. The lawns were like grey velvet. Black shadows tabled across. Here and there, a rim of silver, moon on water. One fountain I could see ceaselessly curving over and over, a stream of liquid spangles—

Somewhere a bird sang a brief little silvery song. They often do on warm nights. And from the river a hippo grunted.

Then a lion roared. They didn't mean anything by it, roaring. Just exercising their lungs. But loud.

Above, all the stars. Would they be different over the Waste?

Perhaps it wasn't really fear I felt. After all, perhaps leaving this place I hated, and which had been so boring and vicious and frankly dangerous for me, I was sad.

When I'd left Jizania, I'd hidden, as you know, and written in this book. I already had all the keys, and the wine for the Guards at the Pavilion, and some things Jizania had told me to get from the Maids' Hall. These included my strongest shoes, which I put on. I'd put everything else in a little bread sack from the kitchens. (Another theft. Several actually. I was even stealing Nemian from them, in a way.)

She'd said I should start at midnight. The clock high up on the House sang out its thin strokes, the only hour it sounds any more.

And I came down to the Garden, and went along towards the Pavilion of Black Marble, approaching from the Upper Shrubberies.

(Jizania had said, it wouldn't do for me to go straight down from her rooms, the way we had earlier. I thought she was sensibly not involving herself any further. But now I wonder if she gave me a last chance to look around, to feel my nerves and my strange regret, to be *sure*.)

However, as I was walking through the hibiscus shrubs, I met a lion.

We both stopped and gaped at each other. It seemed as surprised as I was.

I wasn't sure what to do. It was a *lion*. Of

55

course, I'd seen them out before, but on leads. Anyway, this one was perfectly friendly, or should I say indifferent. It shook its head and padded by, creamy in moonlight, and smelling of the white hibiscus flowers.

When I'd gone on a bit further, though, I looked over from a break in the bushes, and on the Vine Terraces that run down there, lamped by the moon, two other lions, (lionesses) were playing together, rolling over and crushing the vines and the fat grapes, so the air reeked of juice.

On the night Nemian was to escape, the lions had also escaped. If necessary, this would make a splendid diversion.

A coincidence? No, I thought not. Jizania had sent someone else on another errand . . . Hadn't she said she had keys to each lock in the House and Garden – that would include the lions' enclosure.

Doubtless this feat would also be blamed on Claidi. It occurred to me, my name might live on in history here!

Then I could see the wall of the courtyard and the Pavilion cupola over the top.

Well, I felt sick. But somehow I kept walking, and found I'd knocked on the door in the wall. So there was no time to throw up.

One of the Guards spoke harshly through the door.

'Yes? What do you want?'

'To bring you wine, respected Guard.'

56

'Oh. Wine, eh.'

Someone sounded pleased now. Then another one said, 'Who sent it?'

'Her Oldness, Princess Jizania.'

The door was opened, and I pattered through, looking suitably timid and modest.

There were five of them, sitting on benches under a lantern on a pole. They'd been playing cards. Behind them the Pavilion bulked, not a light showing.

I gave them the two large wine bottles, and handed them the two kitchen cups, all I could carry. They didn't seem worried. One of them took a handy undoing-thing out of a pouch and uncorked the bottles.

They passed them around, taking huge sloshing gulps, which was glorious. Jizania had drugged both bottles, I'd seen her do it, inserting a long needle through the corks and letting in some herbal stuff, drip by patient drip.

It didn't work instantly, unfortunately.

'What's in that bundle?'

'Some things the princess sent for the prisoner.'

'What things? What does he want with things? We'll be stringing him up tomorrow, hopefully.'

'Or we'll behead him,' added a particularly jolly one, 'off with that goldy head.'

'Too right, Jovis.'

'Too goldy,' Jovis agreed with himself, thought-fully.

57

I remembered, it was his cannon that had brought down the balloon.

'Here,' said Jovis to me, 'come and sit on my knee, girlie.'

'No, thank you,' I replied politely.

They all laughed, and one kindly explained, 'No, he's not *asking* you, he's *telling* you.'

This sort of thing had happened now and then. I looked coy and half smiled at Jovis the shooter and would-be beheader.

'I'd like to, respected Guard, but I have to get back to my lady. You know how it is.'

'She won't miss you yet.'

I fluttered sweetly, then said, 'I'll just go over and give the horrible prisoner these things she sent him. Then, well, maybe . . . just for a minute. I mean, I've always admired the Guards.'

'Yes,' said Jovis, 'all you girls like us Guards.' Pathetic really, he believed this.

But the wine was strong and they were still gargling it down. They were getting *extra* stupid, having had a head start anyway.

They waved me off to the Pavilion, Jovis promising me how nice it would be when I got back to him.

As I reached the Pavilion, a lion roared – right outside the wall it sounded like.

The Guards chortled. 'Lions're noisy t'night.' And one of them slumped forward and rolled off the bench. The other four looked at him, and it was good old Jovis who declared, 'Carn'old s'wine.'

I turned my back, more confident now, and called softly between the bars of Nemian's cage. I used his name. The first time I had.

At first, no answer. And behind me the Guards still toasting one another, not yet out cold.

Then Nemian spoke to me from the centre of the dark.

'Claidissa?'

My heart jumped. My heart has no sense, really.

I coughed, recovered myself, and said, 'Princess Jizania sent me.'

'Claidissa,' said Nemian again.

So I said fiercely, 'Call me Claidi, please.' Because I couldn't stand it. All this, and *him*, *and* this new name of mine.

There was a clatter and bumping sound. I glanced back. At *last*.

Nemian was suddenly right in front of me, up against the bars.

'God,' said Nemian (another new name – some exclamation they use in the Waste?), 'she did it, she drugged them. It's real then. You're going to get me out. She told me you would. Clever Claidi.'

So I undid the lock, and the bars unfolded, and Nemian stepped out into the moonlit, lion-roaring night.

The Guards were in an unappealing heap. Jovis had his mouth wide open and was dribbling and snoring charmingly. Just what you'd expect of him.

'There are lions outside.'

'Oh, good,' said Nemian.

'They're very tame,' I hoped.

It wasn't far, in any case. And we saw no more lions, only met a small lumbering badger.

(I have a sort of feeling the lions just trotted about for a while, messed the Garden up a bit, and then rambled back into the enclosure.)

I said before that under the Garden were systems of tunnels, where the heating mechanisms were located, tended by slaves. (I said too, the slaves have a rotten time, worse than I'd ever had.)

Jizania had told me how to get down into these tunnels, and how it was simple to go through, if you only took the right-hand turning every time. Travelling like that, from the entry we'd use, we would finally come out beyond the walls—!!

Thinking back again, I have to say I had no qualms about using these tunnels. Crazy. But it just seemed nothing could stop me – us.

Nemian didn't question me either. She must have told him all the plan, before she put it to me. And he must have sat there in the Pavilion-cage, wondering and wondering if I'd have the courage to arrive.

The way in was at a carefully overgrown rocky hill, with trees leaning at the top. I found the door in the ivy, unlocked it, (I suppose she must have copies of all these keys) and went in. Then I lit the first kitchen candle from my bread sack, and put the glass bulb over the top to keep it steady.

Nemian closed the door behind us.

'It's every right-hand turn,' I said. 'I know,' he said. 'And she said,' (me) 'if we pass any of the slaves, take no notice.' 'Well would I,' said Nemian, 'of slaves.'

Somehow that was disturbing, that he said this. I should have expected it. It meant, presumably, that princely Nemian's home-place also has slaves, servants, *maids* – and they don't count for much. Jizania had been very definite in giving him my 'proper' name. 'I've told him you are royal,' she'd said.

But I couldn't think about that, could I, at such a moment.

The tunnels were narrow, dark, and damp in spots, with water trickling down. Here and there they'd been shored up with planks. Here and there too, bricks had fallen out. Not organized picturesque decay, just age and neglect.

After a while we did pass a kind of room, where a vast black furnace stood like a nightmare beast. It wasn't going, because the recent months have been warm.

Later there was another, and a few little holes in the tunnel-sides, and once two slaves were there, but they were fast asleep.

In another area, a fox had got in and made a den. I saw her eyes glow as she glared at us in the candle's light. Bones, too.

After I'd lit the second candle, I began to feel exhausted. I was tired of being in the tunnels. And Nemian treading behind me, once or twice banging his golden head on low rafters or slabs of stone, and cursing, made me more edgy now than excited.

Then I heard the river. Jizania had said I would.

I looked down the passage for the last door the princess had given me a key to.

But when we reached it, the lock was rusty. When I tried to work the key, I couldn't, *couldn't*.

'Let me do it,' he said. His voice was impatient. This managed to make me feel unintelligent and weak and exasperated all together.

But he was flying for his life after all. He'd been offhand about slaves probably for the same reason?

I stood aside, and Nemian, instead of undoing the door as I'd tried to, threw himself against it.

I was quite shocked when it gave way.

It was an old door, rusty and rotted, and outside was the world.

He walked straight out. I . . . followed him.

'But,' I said stupidly. 'The door—'

'No one comes here,' he said.

'But something might get *in*,' I said, 'from – out *there*.'

'*We*,' he said reasonably, 'are out *there*.'

We were.

And in the dark, for the moon was gone, *there* looked no different from the Garden.

The river ran, wide and muscular and dully shining, with tall reeds like iron railings. Rocks piled round us, a lot of them about the door, hiding it quite well, which was lucky since he'd broken it open.

(They'll realize and go and mend the door. The Guards will keep a look-out until it's safe.)

I stared back, and away along the river. I saw the fortressed high walls of the Garden, black on blue-black sky.

Never before had I been this side of them.

My companion had sat down. He said, easily, lightly, 'Did you bring anything to eat, Claidi?'

Flustered, I produced the snacks Jizania suggested I filch from the Maids' Hall kitchens, and set them before Nemian. He didn't seem greatly impressed, but he ate them.

Then he lay back on the ground and I realized he was going to sleep again.

All this time, I'd thought perhaps going to sleep in front of us all in the Debating Hall had been an act, a sort of ploy to seem harmless. But now I think he really can just go to sleep at will, and he does.

He's asleep now. I put out the candle because I was nervous of being spotted – from the walls – from the *Waste*. But it doesn't look like the Waste here.

I watched him a while, but that seemed rude. He *is* very handsome. And – a stranger.

In the end I lit the candle again, what was left of it, and wrote this. I'm bewildered really. I don't know where I am. Literally. Also, he looks wonderful, but I don't know him at all. It's all unknown. And the future. Even myself, now.

HELL?

Next day, I saw the Waste. That was simple enough. The sun rose in front of me, red-orange, hitting my eyes and the rocks behind me. The river burned red. Some birds were calling, in a harsh *different* way. Nemian was still sleeping, like an enchanted prince in one of the library books of the House.

Stiff and chilled, I got up, and walked towards the river, and in a little while I walked along beside it, until the land curved upward to the sun.

As I climbed this slope, I saw a shimmer on the air below the sun's disc. And when I got to the hill's top, I realized the shimmer to be other hills, far off. They were a parched whitish colour. To my right the river coiled away through the hillside and vanished – was gone. Just a steaminess left behind.

Between this area, and the far off, pale and dry-looking hills, was a huge and terrible nothing. I mean, obviously something was there. But the something *was* nothing. A stretch of land – or sand – or dust – with vague shadows in it; and tilted bits the sun was still catching, but no actual *shapes*. Like a tree, a shrub, certainly nothing like a building. Nothing I could recognize.

This seemed to go on for miles and miles, so much further than the Garden land about the House.

I looked back then, the way the exiles sometimes do in the paintings in the Black Marble Corridor.

Dawn bloomed honey and rose against the high walls I had left for ever. Birds were flying over them. It looked safe and gentle and beautiful. But it was a dream, and I'd woken up.

I looked out at the Waste again. I swallowed.

We ate the last of the snacks. There wasn't much. Nemian had had most of it the night before.

He said, uncaringly, 'We should have got further than this, but then, they won't be eager to pursue us. They won't bother, probably. Not out here.' Then he added, 'I'll miss the balloon. But they wrecked it. Then again, I'd have needed ballooneers to get the thing going.'

'Oh, yes?' I said. I didn't understand a word about the balloon.

'I'm no engineer,' said Nemian, seeming pleased he wasn't. 'That's the trouble,' he said, 'always having everything done for you by your servants. We'll be a fine pair. I hope you'll be able to manage, Claidi.'

'Oh, er – I'll try.'

'It isn't going to be a bed of roses, on foot. And I suppose the only exercise you've ever had is dancing, or smacking your pet dog.'

My mouth fell open. This seems to happen a lot now. There are lots of things for it to happen over.

'But I've worked all my life,' I said flatly.

Nemian laughed. 'At your poetry,' he said, 'at working out a riddle. Mmn.'

'No,' I yapped, 'scrubbing floors, running errands, hand-washing linen, grinding face-powder, making—'

He was laughing. Glamorously, of course. His hair in the sun—

'All right,' he said at last. 'Let's pretend you have.'

We went down to the river to fill the flask I'd brought, with clean if rather murky unfiltered water, doubtless with hippo droppings in it.

My mind was rolling about over what he'd said. Apparently Nemian thought I'd been a REAL princess in the House. I was royal, so I'd lived like royalty.

All this while, the walls of the House and the Garden were only about half a mile away, and I became more and more nervous that Guards would march out and arrest us. But no one came. Of course, they wouldn't. However near, we were in the Waste, Hell-on-earth, lost and unreachable.

In the end we set out, up the hill again. At the top, Nemian gazed and sighed. He flicked a look at me.

'If you get tired, Claidi, I'm not going to carry you.'

This was upsetting. Who precisely had rescued him? But I kept quiet now. I was used to keeping quiet before my betters.

On the down slope he spoke again, and used that Waste word: 'For God's sake, I never should have had to put up with *this*.'

After that we marched in silence, Nemian a little ahead of me.

When we reached the plain – if it was – the ground was like screwed-up parchment, sprinkled with powder.

Dusts rose from our footfalls as we walked. We coughed, and then the dust seemed to settle in our throats. We got used to it.

The sun was higher. Far off, the blistered ghosts of the hills. The House walls had disappeared. I'll never see them again.

It was hot. Already.

I have become so used to holding anger at unfairness inside.

And then, well I've told you, I'm in love with him.

And also, here we were, and he seemed to know the way. (Did he?) I knew nothing.

But that first day, it was murder.

In my sack, now tied to my shoulders, the way wrong-doers carry their crimes in the House pictures, bounced this book. I hadn't the heart to write in it, and anyway had no chance, and then was too worn out.

He'd been right. I might be tougher than he reckoned, but I'd *never* had to do anything like this.

The ground was so hard. That sounds stupid. But it was as if, every time you took a step, the ground whacked your feet, and the jolt shot right up your back. The sun thumped down on your head from the other direction.

The landscape was featureless, as it had seemed to be from the hill. There were a few nasty-looking rocks. (They did look nasty, like bad things changed into rocks that might suddenly turn back.)

I saw a lizard. It was pink with a black wiggle on its spine. Nemian never noticed, or he was just used to such sights.

There were some birds in the sky, too, big black ragged things. They seemed interested in us, but then veered away.

We had a rest by a particularly bad-tempered-looking rock at noon. We drank some water, and Nemian went to sleep.

I don't often cry. It doesn't do much good. But I felt rather like it. And then I thought of my parents having to make just this appalling trek. I hoped and hoped they'd succeeded, and got to somewhere, because presumably there *was* somewhere to get to—

If I hoped they'd done it, I must too. I wished, childishly, Nemian had been nicer to me. I wished, instead of saying he wouldn't carry me, (as if I'd have asked) he'd have said, 'Claidi, you've saved my life. We'll see this through. I'll help you.'

But I gazed at his face, and once he had a dream or something and he stirred and frowned and shook his head on the pillow of his rolled-up coat. I leaned over him and whispered, as I used to with Daisy when she had worrying dreams, 'It's all right. Yes, it'll be fine.'

I hope Daisy *is*. And Pattoo, and the others. I'll never know, will I.

That day truly was awful. The land never seemed to alter. The far hills got no nearer.

The sun went over and behind us. At last a glimmering, gold-stitched sunset, with birds arrowing like the stitching needles, hundreds of them it seemed.

Then thankful coolness with the dusk, which quickly turned chilly.

We'd reached a weird place by then. Distance had hidden it that morning, or the slope of the land. There was a small pool in rocks, with a waterfall, quite elegant, the sort of thing they *make* in the Garden. But this pool was a dull ancient green, and the waterfall was the same colour.

'How foul,' said Nemian. 'Whatever you do, don't touch that water. It's undrinkable. Lethal.'

I was thirsty, and starving hungry. Sometimes I'd been made to miss meals (like Daisy) but never all of them for a whole day.

We sat down near the pool. The fall made a soothing noise that somehow stopped being soothing, thinking of the poison. This was just the sort of filthy thing they'd always told me was in the Waste.

However, Nemian took a narrow enamelled box out of a pocket. Undoing the box, he offered it to me. There were little sugary stems in the box.

'Take one,' he said. 'It has all the nourishment you'd get from a roast chicken with vegetables. Or so they always say.' I did take one, cautiously. He did too. He ate it quickly and leaned back on the rock. 'Not as interesting, definitely, as roast chicken. Or do you think it is?'

I crunched the little stem. It tasted spicy and sweet, like one of Jade Leaf's candies. But once it was down, I stopped feeling hungry. And I wasn't tired in quite the same dragging way.

We shared the last water.

'I'm sorry, Claidi,' said Nemian, as the blackening sky filled with whitening stars. 'I'm not, right now, marvellous company. I'm angry at what's happened – but then, I'm also glad, because I've

70

met you. That was something – almost miraculous. You're—' he faltered and so did my pulse. 'You're a wonder, Claidi. Please forgive me for being such a dupp.'

I blinked. What was a *dupp*? Never mind. I was warmer. How bright the stars. He didn't loathe or regret me.

I fell asleep listening to the poison pool, and dreamed I fell in, but Nemian rescued me. The sort of dream it's lovely to have and embarrassing to tell. You know.

Next day, everything changed.

STORMY WEATHER

Sometime I must have half woken. The stars were bright red. I sensibly thought I was dreaming, but I wasn't.

When I woke again, it was daylight.

Only, not really.

Nemian was shaking me. One should never wake anyone like that, unless it's a matter of life and death. But I suppose this was, in fact.

Dust storms had come over the House, but mostly by then blown-out, repelled also by the changed atmosphere, the different climate-in-little of the Garden. They'd never been anything like this.

Slabs of air were tumbling on me like walls.

They were marigold-colour or blood-red, and in between a shifting, spinning greyishness.

Spirals whirled. The light flashed off and on, then was gone, smothered in redness, then broke again like lightning.

You couldn't breathe, or it felt as if you couldn't. I'd put on an out-of-fashion dress for the escape, with a normal skirt. It had a sash too, which now I found Nemian had pulled off and was tying over my nose and mouth. He had done something similar for himself.

But our eyes – how the dust and sand particles stung. And there were spiteful bits of grit.

We crawled among the rocks, trying to find some sort of shelter, but the water was also splashing out from the fall and the pool as the winds stirred them, and Nemian bellowed that we mustn't let this poisonous fluid even touch us. Then somehow we were outside the rocks and couldn't, in the chaos, find them again.

The noise of the dust winds was fearsome. It sounded like something truly terrible, without pity or thought – which it was.

I'd grabbed my little sack – a reflex.

We staggered about, and Nemian grasped my other hand. I find it reassuring to report that, in this situation, I wasn't thrilled when he did that.

He bawled at me we mustn't become separated.

Heads bowed, we tried to push forward. The dust-winds slapped and punched us. Apparently, so

I gathered from his yells, there had been another rocky place further on, which he had spotted as the wind started to build up. This might provide more shelter.

But it was useless. In the end, we crouched down, and covered our heads with our arms. Actually, in his case, only one arm, as he had put the other around me.

At another time, bliss, I suppose. But I was terrified. Not of what the storm could do, exactly, although he said after they can kill, and I believe him. Just of the sheer ferocity of it.

Then, with no warning, the winds – there seemed about six of them – dropped. They fell round us like dry hot washing, and the grit and tiny stones rattled along the ground.

We raised our faces, and saw the strangest – to me – sight.

In House books I'd stolen glances at, I had seen pictures of ancient cities that once had existed in the world before the Waste claimed everything. And this thing I saw now was surely such a city, or its remains.

The land had dropped gradually, and there was a sort of basin, and in this some tall towers with windows, or spaces where windows had been, and ornamented roofs with domes and pedestals. There were pillars too, a whole long line of them that might have stretched for a mile. Mostly there were walls, and carvings, or the bits that were left of them. There was one huge vase, with stone flowers still rising from it.

My eyes streamed, and everything wavered.

I said, 'I never saw that from the higher ground.'

Nemian said, sounding irritated, 'You probably couldn't. The winds uncover things, just as they bury them.'

I'd thought the storm was over, but no. A second or so more, having shown me the city ruins as if to educate me, and the whole thing started up again.

How long it lasted this time I can only make a guess. It felt like hours. Finally I was lying on the ground. I cringe to say it, but I think I was whimpering. Well, maybe I wasn't. Just grunting. Anyway Nemian was utterly still. And once everything stopped, I was afraid he'd smothered completely.

But he sat up, and shook himself, and combed handfuls of white and yellow dust out of his hair with both hands.

I have this ridiculous idea, only it couldn't be, could it? He'd *gone to sleep again*. Didn't dare ask.

I stood up, and shook out my skirt and my own hair, and then gave up. (I must, I thought, look like Nemian, as if I'd been damped and dipped in flour.)

When I looked around, the city ruin was gone again. The dip in the plain had become a mound.

Presently, about an hour later, when we walked up it, I stumbled on one stone blossom still sticking up from the buried vase.

Nemian made no mention of having taken my hand, or seeming to try to protect me. He scowled at the Waste, then his face simply became smooth and beautiful again. (His hair had lost its glory, though.)

He said, 'Well done for bringing the water flask.' (It was in the sack.) And then, 'Reliable Claidi.'

But I'd grabbed the sack because it had this book in it. The flask, after all, was empty.

There were so many questions I should have asked, aren't there. I bet you would have. You would have said, for instance, *Where exactly are we going?* And *What will happen to me when we get there?* And you might have insisted he knew that, though Claidi was perhaps half royal, she'd lived first as a dogsbody and floor polisher, and next as Jade Leaf's maid-slave.

I didn't ask or say anything much. I'm not completely making an excuse. For one thing, I was so *tired*. Compared to this tiredness, my other tired times in the House seemed nothing.

Someone else would have been upheld by a sense of excitement and optimism. But I felt exasperated a lot. With the Waste mainly. And with Nemian. And with me.

The sun got higher and hotter and more unbearable, and I was desperate to have a drink of water. One doesn't realize how awful thirst is until something like this happens, worse than hunger.

After the buried city was behind us the land was very bumpy, and yet totally the same. Crash went the ground, hitting my feet.

Far, far off, still no nearer, the pale parched hills which looked, anyway, most uninviting.

We reached a rock, one rock, but it threw a shadow. So we sat down in the shadow.

Nemian stretched out his long legs. His clothing had been perfect, but wasn't now.

'You've been very strong,' he said to me, 'not drinking any water.'

'There isn't any.'

I'd thought he knew.

'Oh,' he said. He frowned. 'Didn't you bring any?'

'Yes. You – we drank it.'

'Well, yes. But I thought there was more. I thought you understood, this might be a long journey. Didn't the princess tell you?'

Had she? I didn't think she had. I suppose it was common sense and I was just a twit. Then again, I couldn't have carried much more. He would have carried it, maybe.

Nemian took the enamelled box out of his pocket. He offered me another of the sugary stalks.

The stalk was difficult to chew with such a dry mouth and scorched dusty throat.

But it did help. Even the thrist became more uncomfortable than sharply painful.

'You see,' said Nemian, 'there is a town over

there somewhere,' he waved idly at the hills. 'I saw it from the balloon. We can get transport there, perhaps. Unless they're very unfriendly. Which they may be.'

I'd thought everyone and thing was unfriendly in the Waste. But Nemian had come from the Waste.

He closed his eyes. I heard myself say in a faint panic: 'Don't—'

'Don't? What?'

I wanted to say, Don't go to sleep. Talk to me, please. But what right did I have to demand that?

When I didn't add anything, he shrugged and – slept.

Glumly I sat there.

I tried to be brave. I tried to think he was wise to sleep, and I should try to as well. But the sugary spice-stalk seemed to have made me wide awake in addition to staying tired.

So I sat and stared nervily out over the plain.

Little spirals of dust still spun there. Huge hollow clouds above. A large black bird hung motionless on the air, as if from an invisible rope.

He'd only held my hand and put his arm around me to keep us together. He had felt responsible, like a kind prince for his servant. And I'd let him down. Hadn't brought enough water.

I thought if anyone in the House had been the way he was it would have annoyed me. Because it was Nemian, I felt in the wrong. Was this a very bad sign?

A huge new blond cloud was streaming along the plain. Getting bigger.

I watched it, then properly saw it. Before I considered I jumped up with a howl.

Nemian woke.

'Are you a girl or some species of jumping deer?'

'The storm – it's started again!'

He looked, with those cool eyes.

'No, it isn't the storm. Riders, and vehicles.'

And he sprang to his feet and ran, all in one coordinated bound, across the plain away from me, towards the dust cloud.

Had I been abandoned? Was I expected to follow? I'd better follow, hadn't I?

I floundered into a panting gallop.

The cloud (riders and vehicles) was going from right to left across the near horizon, slightly looping in towards us as it went. Because the ground was fairly flat now, I didn't see at first they were on a sort of makeshift road which the storm had obviously uncovered.

How far was it to reach them? Miles. Probably not. Towards the end I had to keep stopping, gasping for breath, but by then some of them had slowed down, and then halted.

When I eventually staggered up, Nemian was in conversation with seven brown men in the two halted vehicles. The others had gone rolling on.

There was a *mad* noise. This was because the two chariots (I recognized them from the riding vehicles the princes sometimes used in the Garden) were drawn, each, by a team of six, very large, curl-horned sheep. Some of the sheep were bleating in deep voices. And then I grasped the chariot riders were also bleating. And Nemian was bleating too.

For a minute I thought I'd lost my mind. Or they all had.

Then Nemian turned and saw me standing there with my hair raining down and my mouth as usual wide open.

He smiled, and raised one eyebrow.

'Hello, Claidi. You needn't have rushed. These are Sheepers. I know their language.'

One of the brown men, who wore their hair in plaits, braided, like the wool of the sheep teams, with beads and sheep-brasses, said loudly, 'B'naaa?'

Nemian turned back, and bleated in return.

A few moments more, and one of the riders in the second chariot got out, and jumped into the first chariot. Helping hands drew Nemian and me into the second chariot.

Everything smelled very oily and woolly. But — oh wonderful — a leather bottle was being offered to us. Nemian politely let me drink first. It wasn't water but warmish sheep milk, and I wasn't terribly delighted. But it did soothe my throat.

'We're going to the Sheeper town,' Nemian informed me.

A whip cracked high, well clear of woolly backs, and we were off.

CHARIOT TOWN

There was quite a welcome.

Under a square gateway in a thick wall, but only just high enough so we could drive through, and into the brown town of the Sheepers. And everyone had come out, in the dusk, with lamps. Women laughing and holding up babies, and children screaming and bouncing, and old men leaning on wooden staffs, and grannies (they call them that), old women, and almost all of them were banging drums and blowing whistles, and some even threw flowers – a particularly *hard* sort of white poppy.

I gathered, but not right then, the chariot-riding Sheepers had been off somewhere, trading. With some other settlement of Sheepers? Anyway, it was a success. Best of all, the road had reappeared after the storm, which made the journey quicker. Although in fact we'd ridden with them until after sunset.

As the sky flamed, the hills had abruptly seemed to come nearer, then the sheep chariots bundled round a swerve in the road, and we saw the town lying in the curve of two really near, rounded low hills, as if in the paws of a lion.

They call it, not for the sheep, as they do practically everything else, but for their chariots. Chariot Town.

Nemian says the walls may belong to something older and lost. The Sheepers patched them up and built inside.

The houses are made of wood and skins. (*Not* sheep. They *never* kill sheep.) Each has a strange little open garden, a stretch of neat close-cut fawn turf.

In the middle of the town is a bigger garden, green in parts, with some trees. Water wells up from the ground into a string of pools. The water's clean. (Except for what the sheep do in it, of course.)

When not employed, the sheep simply wander about the town. Everyone pats them, or gets out of their way, and even if they eat the washing, they're allowed to. They also stroll in and out of everyone's houses, and sometimes leave sheep pats, but these are used for kindling on the fires. (So are useful.)

People groom their sheep carefully, and plait ribbons and beads in their wool. Sometimes they paint their horns.

The sheep are shod. Otherwise they provide wool, milk and cheese. (Which is quite good, once you get used to it. I *think* I have.)

The Chariot Towners can talk to the sheep, (?) and apparently the sheep can talk to them, (?) (all baaing). They do seem to understand each other with no trouble.

The guest-house, where we've been staying, is hung with sheep-brasses. And at night they light candles in the skulls of famous old sheep which died peaceful natural deaths. All the houses own such skulls. They're heirlooms.

The sheep graze the lawns, that's why they're so neat, the lawns not the sheep.

The lord here is called the Shepherd.

Look, I've gone on and on about sheep.

You catch that, here.

I've written everything up now to date.

We've been in the town five days.

Nemian *talked* to me today. I don't always see him, except at breakfast and/or supper. (Mounds of cheeses, milk-soups, salads, gritty bread. Beer. (Which gives me hiccups, to add to the bad impression I make.)) Then he chats in baaas to the locals.

He said, when speaking to me, I was being 'astonishingly patient'. Some choice.

Nemian is out all day, with the Sheepers. He mentioned other travellers come and go here, and soon we should be able to hitch a ride to somewhere else, perhaps where there are balloons and ballooneers. So *home*. (To wherever his home is.) The Sheepers like him. Of course.

Desolate.

That sounds yukky. Just like some swooning princess of the House. *Ooh, I'm sooo desolate—*

But I am.

I wander about and try to talk to some of the women milking sheep or making sheep–cheese or grooming sheep, or their kids. But we can't understand each other. I find I must simply amble past, and give a quick cheery bleat, which they seem to take as a well-mannered and pleasant Hallo.

Nemian looks amazing again. We're able to wash our hair and have baths here, though the water is rather cold (one heated bucket to three not.) He's dazzled them.

He did say the sheep are fierce and can fight lions. (Do they kick them with their shoes?)

Yes, we too have talked about the sheep.

Depressing.

Have now been here eight days, also depressing.

Depressed.

I'm fed up with me. How can I be depressed. I'm OUT IN THE WASTE. With NEMIAN. Almost.

Depressed.

My God – I know what that means, sort of – and shouldn't perhaps use it like that (?)

83

Daisy and Dengwi used to accuse me of being prissy, because I wouldn't swear.

But the royalty at the house used to swear, and I hated them, so I didn't want to do anything they did and which I could avoid doing.

(If Nemian swears, it doesn't seem so awful, I have to confess.)

And God is a kind of supreme supernatural figure. *Not* human. I don't really understand. But I've caught the phrase from him, as I've caught this habit of talking about the sheep . . .

Anyway. Nemian took me aside this evening. And it was sensational. We actually had a conversation, and for hours.

It began with supper. The rough wood tables are outside on a trip-you-up terrace of piled stones. The air was clear and fresh and the sky got dark very slowly.

Everyone baa'd away. I sat there resignedly, only nodding with a quick smiling bleat when anyone greeted me: 'Claaa-di-baa!'

When it got to the serious beer-drinking stage, Nemian rose and said to me, 'Shall we go for a walk, Claidi? It's a fine night.'

One or two of the Sheepers grinned and looked away. And I felt myself blush, which was infuriating. So I said, blankly, 'Oh, I'm a bit tired. I think I'll just go in—' wishing I'd shut up.

'Let me persuade you,' said Nemian, very gracious. 'We can go up to the water pools. It's cool there. We have to talk, don't we?'

'All right,' I charmingly snapped, got up, and stalked away up the terrace towards the big garden further along the track. Let Nemian catch up with *me*, for a change.

He didn't bother, of course. So then I had to pretend I'd got a stone in my shoe. It could have been true, my shoes are wearing out fast.

He sauntered up and asked me, all concern, 'A stone?'

'Oh, I've shaken it out now.'

'Look,' said Nemian, 'there's the moon.'

We looked. And there it was. Since the storm it hadn't properly been visible. Now it looked clean and white, a half round, like half a china clock-face, but without hands or numbers.

'Poor Claidi,' said Nemian. 'Are you very angry with me? I've been selfish, haven't I?'

I had to remind myself here that although he is a prince, he thinks I'm a princess, at least a lady.

'Everyone's selfish,' I said. 'We have to be. How else can you get by.'

'My God, that's a judgement,' said Nemian. 'But you could be right. Can you forgive me, then, since you never expected anything much from me in the first place?'

I stole a look at him. Wonderful.

'Oh, yes,' I said, as firmly as I could.

We walked into the garden.

The trees grouped around the pools, and the moon shone in each scoop of water, as we went by.

He found a smooth stone, where the white poppies grew, giving off a ghostly musk in the moon-watered dark.

'You see,' he said, 'I never expected the balloon to be shot down. Most of the places I passed over were so primitive they didn't have the means. I thought anywhere that was sophisticated, would also have balloons itself. Perhaps be used to travellers. But then all those guns went off, and I thought I was going to be killed.' He looked across the garden, bleakly. 'It shook me up. And then – quite a reception your people gave me.'

'You didn't seem . . .' I hesitated, 'upset at all.'

'Oh come on, Claidi. That was an act. All noble and dashing. I was at my wits' end.'

'So you lay down on the floor in front of everyone and went to sleep.'

He frowned and cast me one slanting look.

'Actually, I passed out. I'd had a thump on the head getting into the tree. Rather than just fall over flat, I did it that way, noble and dashing again, and *very* careless. An act. I said.'

I was amazed. I felt strange. I can't describe it. I'm not sure I'd want to. I admired him, too. And – I felt guilty. Those times on the journey when he'd simply gone to sleep – had he been feeling ill? And he hadn't trusted me, or was too proud to show it.

'Anyway,' he now said. 'I owe you my life.' (The words I'd wanted before.) 'I won't forget that, Claidi. I have an important position in my own city. You're going to have wonderful experiences there. You'll live in a luxury beyond anything in that House. And you'll be respected and honoured.'

All this sounded so bizarre, I couldn't take it in. Me? I didn't really care anyway. Just liked him to go on talking.

So then he told me things about his city. I was impressed. Apparently it far outshines the ruin we'd glimpsed. A mighty river runs through, a mile or more wide, so in places you can't see across from one bank to the other. The water is pure as glass. The buildings rise to vast heights, and are so tall they have sort of clockwork cages in them, they call lifters, which carry people from the ground floor to the top storey.

He said they'd let off fireworks in celebration to welcome him home, and to greet me. I've heard of fireworks, but never seen them. He said they're the colours of a rainbow, shot with gold and silver stars.

He said the city is governed from four great towers. The most powerful tower is the Tower of the Wolf. And he was born in this tower.

Then I remembered something he'd said in the Debating Hall, about being on a search or quest.

I asked him what that was. Nemian laughed. 'Oh, I was just making it sound grand. I was only travelling.'

I asked him where the red flowers grew, like the one he'd given to Jizania Tiger.

'In my city,' he said. 'We call them Immortals. After you pick them, they can live for months, even without water. You see, Claidi, even here the Waste isn't all a desert. And there are places where everything's – like your Garden. Only far better. Cooped up in that House, you must have found it very dull. You must have been very bored.'

'It was all rules and senseless Rituals,' I muttered.

'I can guess. Rules should *never* be boring,' he oddly replied.

Then he leaned over and kissed me lightly on the lips.

I was so stunned, that it meant almost nothing as it happened. So I have to keep recalling it, re-living it, that kiss. Trying to feel its staggering importance.

In a funny way it makes me think of when I scalded myself once, as a child. For some moments I didn't feel a thing.

I'm still waiting to feel this. I know when I do, it will be colossal, sweeping through me, like the pain of the scald, only not pain at all.

After he'd kissed me, we went on talking, as if nothing at all had happened.

He knows so *much*. But then, I know *nothing*.

My head's bursting now with sketches of other places in the Waste, towns, cities, places where they use hot-air balloons for flight.

A couple of times, people had passed, more or less unnoticed by me. But then some sheep came wandering by, and after them some couples, saying to us shyly, 'Brur'naa-baa,' which apparently, (Nemian) means something like 'Are we disturbing you?' And since they seemed awkward, and it's their garden, we got up and walked back to the guest-house.

When I'd climbed up the ladder, (no lifters here) to my narrow bed, piled with woollen blankets and scented by sheep, I was frozen.

Since I couldn't sleep at all, I've sat and written this down, and now I think that may be dawn, that light low in the window – or is it?

After I went down the ladder again, I peered over the sort of gallery there, where a famous sheepskull called *Praaa* burns a big candle all night.

Coming into the guest-house was a crowd of men, mostly young. They were dressed in rather a fantastic way, skin trousers, tunics, boots, jackets with gilded buttons and tassels, and whirling cloaks. They had a lot of weapons, knives and bows, and a couple of rifles.

The Sheepers were baaing and bowing.

Candlelight pranced on wild tanned faces.

I wondered if Nemian knew about this, and if it was going to be useful.

But really, they looked, the newcomers, like accounts I'd heard mumbled in tales in the House. Wandering bands of bandits from the Waste, criminals, who'd stab you as soon as say hallo.

I crept back up the ladder and huddled into bed.

Of course, the House told lies about the Waste. The Waste isn't like anything I was told – or not all of it. Or not all of what I've seen so far.

Finally I did go to sleep, because I was woken by a riotous row downstairs.

Was it the bandits? What were they doing? Murdering everyone and about to set fire to the guest-house?

I scrambled up and got dressed, but just then one of the Sheeper women came in, bleated, and handed me some milk and a piece of bread.

You can imagine I wanted to ask her what was going on, but I couldn't speak the baa-language, and pointing anxiously at the floor and straining my eyebrows up and down, only seemed to make her think *I* thought there were mice in the room. She hurried about looking under the wool rugs, found nothing, and bleating reassuringly, went out all smiles.

Presumably as she'd brought the breakfast and was smiling, nothing too awful was taking place.

I ate. Then washed my hair in what was left of last night's washing water. I did it for something to do, really. The day was already hot, and I was soon almost dry. Someone knocked.

It was one of the Shepherd's men. He put a small chunk of wood into my hand. I bleat-thanked him and stood there stupidly. Then he pointed at the wood, and I saw something had been scratched on it. The Sheepers didn't have paper. Their writing seemed to have something to do with the patterns they make with the beads and things on the sheep . . .

Anyway, the scratches read, 'Go with him. Bring everything you want. We're leaving at once.'

I gulped. 'From Nemian?' I asked.

'N'baa miaan'baa,' said the man. Or something like that. But nodding.

There wasn't much now to pack in the sack. This book, of course, the ink pencil I write with, the flask, even though I hadn't had a chance to refill it. A few bits and pieces.

I was scared. I had to face it now, the Waste still frightens me. Although apparently full of towns and tribes and settlements and even 'sophisticated' cities, there were all those deserts and poisonous areas in between.

No time for qualms. I climbed down the ladder after the Sheeper.

In the main indoor room, where usually we'd eaten breakfast, the loud noise was going full tilt.

Men were roaring and laughing, and someone was singing, and plates were smashing or just being used very roughly. Through a doorless doorway I caught a rush of tan cloak, flaming with gold fringes.

We went along the gallery, through a side door, and down an outside wooden stair.

In the dirt-floored side yard, a chariot had been hitched up with a team of four sheep, with painted horns.

Nemian stood in the chariot with the driver. He made a brisk princely movement with one arm, hurrying me to come over and get in.

'Nemian, I didn't fill—'

'Shut up, Claidi.'

Nice.

Oh well. This was obviously not the time for a chat. If he wasn't the gentlemanly joy he'd been last night, we could just be in danger right now.

We left the yard slowly, not making much sound. I don't think the rowdy bandits would have heard us anyway.

I could hear *them*.

Bash went something, and *slam* went something else, and gales of happy laughter, and someone crying more or less in the language Nemian and I spoke, 'You kill it properly, Blurn. Don't try to eat it alive.'

Oh . . . *God*, I thought.

Outside the yard the whip cracked, and the sheep, thank Whoever, kicked up their shod hoofs.

We went at quite a lick down the main track, and not long after were let swiftly out by the gate of Chariot Town, at the feet of the pale hills.

TROUBLE ALWAYS FOLLOWS

Pattoo used to say, solemnly, 'If you run away from trouble, it always follows.'

Rather my impression, too. Though that never stopped me trying.

It's certainly what happened that morning.

After the first bolt up the rattling hill slope, the going got very steep. We had to slow down.

But looking back from quite a high spot, you could see some of the town, and the gate, and nothing was going on there.

Nemian and the chariot driver had baa'd a bit. Now Nemian said to me, 'You realize why we left?'

'They were dangerous, the men who arrived.'

'According to the Sheepers, that's putting it mildly,' said Nemian. 'They're all mad, those wandering people. Theirs is a hell of a life.' He smiled. 'Tempting, really. To live by skill and courage. One long adventure. But pretty foul too. No comforts. And they can't afford any politenesses.'

Neither had he, I thought. Which summed it up. In constant danger lay constant rudeness. What an extremely petty thought.

It's just . . . Well, I've had enough of people treating me like rubbish. I'd innocently thought that would change. And last night—

Last night was apparently last night.

The sheep trotted for a while, where the ground levelled, then clambered, the chariot lurching, on the steeper parts.

I couldn't be bothered to explain now how I'd had no chance to fill the water flask. I suppose I could have used the hair-wash-water, all soapy, with hairs in it. Hmm.

'Don't sulk, Claidi,' said Nemian. 'Did you like it there so much? How silky your hair looks today.'

'Where are we going to now?' I asked with thin dignity.

'The Sheeper will see us on to a hill village up here. We'll have to find our own way from there. There may be a cart or something we can barter for.'

I knew about barter, the exchanging of one thing for another, although in the House it never happened. *Buying* things didn't either, but I'd heard of that too, and Nemian had mentioned (last night) that his city on the wide river used coins, money.

The Sheepers hadn't seemed to want any returns. They just seemed friendly. I hoped that would keep them safe with the bandit band.

The hills were opening out all around us now, and weren't as ugly as I'd anticipated. Very little grew on them, however. An occasional bush with whitish fluff, a type of short pale grass. In the closer distance, they looked soft, like pillows.

We pulled up after about an hour, and the sheep chomped the grass. Nemian and the Sheeper shared some beer, but I didn't fancy it.

I was looking back down the hills, when I heard – we all heard – a beating *clocking* sound ringing from the hills' backs.

Suddenly, over a slope to the left, prescisely where we didn't expect them, five men appeared, less than a quarter of a mile off.

I managed an especially unsuitable idiot question.

'What are *those*?'

'Horses,' said Nemian. 'And the others, *on* the horses, are the mad knife-men from the town.'

I noted no one was trying to start the sheep and chariot. Then I realized we'd never get away. For the bandits had seen us, and I saw their white grins flash, as all the buckles and bangles and buttons and *knives* were doing. They smacked the horses' sides lightly, and these new beasts came racing at us, like a wind or a fire.

(I've never seen a horse before that. In the House the chariots were drawn by – you've guessed – slaves.

They're rather beautiful, aren't they, if you know horses. The long heads and the hair flowing back, just as the bandits' long hair flowed back.)

In about ten seconds, so it seemed, there they

were on the hillside with us, all reds and tans, and metal-and-tooth flash.

'Couldn't let you go,' said one, 'without saying Hi.'

They laughed. They had an accent, intense, gutteral, and somehow extra threatening.

Their politeness was unsettling not because it wasn't real, but because, as Nemian had said, they wouldn't afford politeness.

Nemian, now, said nothing.

The Sheeper didn't seem talkative either.

The horses were polished as any floor.

One of the bandits swung off his horse. He walked over on long legs.

'Not from these parts?'

Nemian said, 'No.'

'South? Peshamba?'

Nemian said, 'Yes, we're heading for Peshamba.'

The bandit leaned on the side of our chariot, companionable. From inside his shirt he drew a small glassy thing, some sort of charm? He gazed down at it in silence, as if all alone. How odd. Another bandit, still mounted, craned over as if to see. This other one gave a sudden whoop (which made me jump). He drew out his (ghastly) knife and flipped it in the air, catching it gently in his *teeth*.

The bandit leaning on the chariot took no notice. He closed the charm in his fist and put it away. Then he looked straight into my eyes.

His were dark, like his long hair that hung to his

waist. He was the colour of strong tea with a dash of milk. A colour that toned well with the horse he'd ridden. I'd thought he would be older. I never saw anyone so − I don't know what to say − *Terrible*.

I shrank.

To my surprise, he at once looked away, and right at Nemian now.

'Any money on you?'

'Money,' said Nemian.

'They use it in Peshamba, or whatever big place you're headed for,' helpfully explained the bandit.

'You want some money,' guessed Nemian. From one of his host of pockets he took a flat leather case, and offered it to the bandit.

The bandit accepted it, opened it.

The bandit and I both stared with curiosity at the weird turquoise-green leaves of paper which were revealed.

Then the dark *eyes* glanced at me sidelong. I felt sick and sidled back.

'Right,' said the bandit. 'Well I can't use this.' (He sounded as if he was saying it wasn't good enough!) 'Any coins?'

'Sorry,' said Nemian. He didn't seem worried. Just well-mannered and willing to talk, as though the mad bandit killers were perfectly normal people met in a garden.

One of the other bandits, (not the one with the knife) called, 'Tell the tronker to shake out his coat. And what's that bird got hidden?'

Tronker? Bird?

The chariot-leaning bandit gave him a casual look.

'I don't think they're good for much,' he pityingly said. Oh, we'd let him down properly.

'Come off it, Argul,' said the other bandit. '*She's* all right, that bird, eh?' (Ah. The 'bird' was me.)

All the old tales raced through my bubbling mind. Horrible stories, with death at the end of them.

But I glared up at the talking bandit on the horse. I felt so terrified I thought I was going to be sick or cry, but instead I screamed at him, '*You touch me and I'll bite your nose off!*'

There was a shocked silence.

Then all at once they all burst out laughing.

This included the chariot-leaning bandit, the other four bandits, and Nemian. *Nemian!*

Even the Sheeper was smiling – perhaps thinking we'd all now be best friends.

And I was appalled. What had I said – done—

Nevertheless my fingers had curled. My nails felt strong and sharp. How revolting it would be to bite that bandit – but my teeth were snapping.

I'd slapped Jade Leaf, I'd escaped the House. I won't be stopped, not any more.

The bandit called Argul shifted away from the chariot. 'Better watch out,' he told the other bandits, 'she means what she says.' He handed the leather container with money back to Nemian. 'I can see,' said Argul to Nemian, 'you've got enough on your hands with that bird you've got there. She scares *me* all right.'

'Yes, yes,' warbled the other bandits, 'he's got real problems there.'

Then the bandit leader spun round, ran at his horse, so I thought he meant to knock it right over, and leaped – *leaped* – up the side of it, as if it were only a little still rock.

Next second he was astride the horse. And unruffled, the horse looked down at me from a dark smooth eye.

'So long,' cheerfully called the bandits, 'have a lovely day!' as they galloped away back down the hill.

We didn't get to the hill village until late in the afternoon.

Nemian said nothing about the bandits. He had said all he wanted, earlier, when he told me they were mad.

Somehow I kept thinking they'd appear again, mad minds changed, to rob, terrify, shame and slaughter us. They didn't.

We had some sheep cheese and lettuce and some beer. I got hiccups.

I was fed up. In a mood, as Daisy used to say.

The sky turned deep gold and we rumbled over yet one more hill-top, and there was the village. It wasn't a thrilling sight. Huddles of lopsided huts all over the place, a huge rambling rubbish tip you could smell from far off. Dogs wandered, snarling. A few sullen human faces were raised to glare at us.

It was as unlike the friendly Sheepers' town as seemed possible, as if specially formed to be off-putting.

Well, I think it was. I'm writing this last section at night, in a sort of barn place, which stinks and is full of enormous rats. Actually the rats are rather handsome, better than the hill-villagers. Quite easy, that.

They behaved foully as soon as we got there. Some stared at us in the sheep-chariot, and some just went in. They'd have banged their doors if they could, but such doors as they have would have fallen off.

Presently a fat gobbling sort of man arrived and baa'd at the Sheeper. Nemian said to me he baa'd so badly the Sheeper obviously could hardly understand, and Nemian not at all.

Even so the Sheeper told Nemian – baaing properly – that we'd 'be all right here'. And yes, they'd let us have a cart with a mule – what is that? – either tomorrow or the day after.

They are called Feather Tribe. They like birds?

Naturally they wanted paying? No, said the Sheeper, apparently. I saw he looked embarrassed. He had to leave us here (to go back to his own so-much-pleasanter place). Nemian didn't comment. I couldn't.

We got out, and the Sheeper went into a hut with the awful fat gobbly person. (Later the Sheeper reappeared loaded with sacks of something, got in his chariot and went off, not even waving good-bye.) Nemian and I were sort of shovelled, by a couple of revolting women, into one of the barns. This one.

I thought Nemian would throw up at once. His face went white and his eyes went white and his nostrils *curled*.

'Oh, Claidi. What can I say. What will you think?'

'It's not your fault,' I said. Grudgingly, I have to admit. I didn't think it *was* his fault. But in a way it was. I mean, he'd gone 'travelling', and then involved us both in all this. I really mean I was angry with him. Love is like this, so the songs of the House used to say. You adore them one minute. Then want to throttle them.

Anyway, he didn't hang about. He left me sitting on the smelly straw, and went to find someone to do something. He didn't come back.

At first I wasn't worried. Then I was worried. Going to the barn door, I then saw Nemian in conversation with the gobbly fat one. (Nemian must speak this language too.) They were both drinking something and yowling away with amusement. Typical.

I sat on the stony ground outside the barn.

Soon a dog wandered up and bared yellow fangs

at me for no reason. Stupidly, I snapped, 'Oh stop it, you fool.' Then I thought it'd leap for my throat. But it whined and ran off with its tail on the ground.

Nemian and the GFO – their leader? – went striding off, on what looked like a tour of the village. (This dung-heap goes back to my grandmother's day. This hole in the roof was made by my great grandfather's pet pigeon, which ate too much, and so fell through.)

A woman came up near evening, and plunked a bowl down beside me.

'Er – excuse me – what is it?' I fearfully asked.

'Germonder pop,' said she. Or so it seemed.

I tried the germonder pop. And it was OBSCENE. So no dinner for Claidi.

There are no lamps in the barn, though the huts lit up later. The moon is very bright, and I've written this by the light of it.

The village-Feather-Tribe are making dreadful sounds. Are they eating, or talking, or what? It's sickening.

(I saw Nemian again, about an hour ago. He wandered by with the GFO and saluted me. He seemed happy, enchanted by these Featherers, some of whom were now trailing him in a merry group. Was he drunk, or just being tactful? Or is he . . . is he useless? When the bandits were there, I never felt for one moment Nemian could save me, as in the old stories the hero always does the heroine – but am I even a heroine? Some chance.)

Retreated back into barn. I might as well go to sleep. Deadly day. Yes, of course I should be glad and pleased I'm on this big adventure. But I have to assure you, the smell in here is enough to make the boldest flinch.

Outside, it seems to be getting brighter and noisier. The moon? Is the moon noisy? Who knows.

Keep thinking of that glass charm the bandit had, the one who leaned on the chariot.

I think they were the end, being so insulting about me (bird! Problems!) when I was only desperate to defend myself, which nobody else would.

FLIGHT

The roof goes up so high, it's hard to believe it's a wagon. The bumping helps, though, to remind me.

It's difficult to write here. I'll leave this, I think, until we stop.

Have to note the colours in the roof. Deepest crimson, and purple with wild greens. The pictures are of horses and dogs, mostly. And a sun done in raw gold, dull with time.

They've had these wagons for ever.

Bump.

I'll wait.

When I'd been asleep in the Feather Tribe's barn just long enough to be confused if woken, and not long enough to have had a rest, thumps and yodels started and someone was shaking me. (I believe I said before that's a terrible way to wake anyone.)

I shot up, and there were all these Feather Tribe people, looking entirely changed. That is, they were beaming and nodding at me, and one of them was flapping a feathery thing about in front of me, like an enormous wing.

Not amazingly, I sat staring.

Then Nemian appeared through the crowd.

'It's all right, Claidi. It's a gift.'

'What? What is?'

'That dress.'

'Is it a dress?'

'It's made out of feathers sewn on wool. It'll be rather hot. I'm sorry. But they seem to want you to have it. There's some sort of festival tonight.'

'Oh.'

'They want us to go with them to some shrine in the hills.'

'What's a *shrine*?'

'Don't worry now. The women will dress you, and then we'll go with them. We need their help, don't we, so we have to join in, be gracious.'

I was only more bewildered by this explanation.

104

Anyway, he and the men had gone, and there were only these four or five large women intent on putting me into the feather-dress. I'd been clothed by force quite often in childhood. I knew it was safer not to resist.

My God, (am I using that right? Think so – seems to be a sort of exclamation used in alarm or irritation) that dress. I think I looked like a gigantic white chicken. Also, it *was* hot, and it itched.

Having clad me, the women were leading me to the door, but I snatched up my bag when I saw one of them fumbling with it.

Supposing they could read? And read *this*? (Which was far fetched. They barely seemed able to talk.)

Outside the whole village had assembled with torches.

They were clapping their hands, and now started to sing. I think it was singing.

Frankly I wasn't sure if I preferred this jolly festive side to them. I preferred the scowling stand-offish way they'd been earlier. Now they kept touching my arms and hair, or my back, and I hated it.

I shouted at Nemian, but he only waved. He was with the GFO, at the procession's front. I say procession, since this is what it became.

We walked quite briskly out of the village, and up a stony track into the hills.

A few dogs ran after and the festive villagers threw stones at them until they turned back. Sweet people. No wonder the dogs were so dodgy and also cowed.

These hills are strange. The whole of the Waste is strange, of course, to me. But all the parts are bizarre in different ways. They all have a different character.

The hills . . . are like a place where something intense, perhaps heavy, had been, which now was blown away. They had a weird beauty in the moon-and-torchlight. Where the grass is thick, the hillsides seem covered with velvet, and then bare pieces strike through, harsh and hard. Also there are bits that are worn thin, translucent, and you seem to see through them, down into darkness.

It was all uphill.

The Gobbly Fat One, who was lord, had to keep having a breather, so then we all got one. They passed round a putrid drink. Luckily, when I shook my head, no one forced me to try it.

Inappropriately I recalled climbing all the stairs of the high tower at the House. Perhaps when we got to wherever we were going, the view would be worth the climb.

And it was.

Suddenly we were up on a broad flat table of land.

They all gave a glad bellow, and stamped and clapped and 'sang' again, and more drink went round, and I thought if they kept pushing it past and breathing it over me, I'd probably puke all over them, and serve them right.

But then they drew off, and I looked up.

A colossal sky was overhead, the biggest sky I'd ever seen. It was quite *blue*, with mottled wisps of cloud, but mostly encrusted by masses of diamond stars. In the midst of it, the moon was at its highest point, so white it burned, and held in a smoky, aquamarine ring.

Dizzy, I looked down. The hills had drawn back, and in front there was nothing but the moon-bleached flat of land which seemed to stop in mid-air.

I thought, I bet it drops off there, into a chasm.

This was correct.

Over to one side there were some caves, and the Feather Tribe villagers were scrambling into them with raucous yells.

You can guess, I wasn't keen to follow, and no one insisted.

To take my mind off the itchy feather dress, I gazed up again at the stars.

I felt I could float right out of myself, and up to them, and in among the drifts of night there would be adventures beyond anything ever found below.

When I looked back this time, Nemian was there, gazing at me. 'You have such a graceful neck,' he said to me.

All the starry adventures faded. I was happy to be in this one.

'Thank you.'

'The stars are wonderful, aren't they,' he said. And then, 'But I'd think your favourite time would be dusk.' He hesitated and said, 'Because of your mother.'

A lot of noise was coming from the caves, and down the slopes behind us, I could hear some (big?) animal scuffling, and who knew what sort of animal, out here. But all that was instantly rinsed off my mind.

'My mother?'

'Because,' he said, 'of her name. Twilight.'

I stood there. 'I didn't – know.'

He said, 'But – didn't you? I understand you lost her when you were young, but even so—'

I must pretend something. I was a princess of the House. Of course I knew my mother's name. Or, why pretend?

I said, 'No one told me. Who told *you*?'

'The Princess Jizania told me.'

And not me? Had she forgotten to?

I said humbly, feeling numb with *feeling*, 'It's a good name.'

(Nemian was frowning, about to ask something. I braced myself.)

At that moment the Featherers began to erupt out of the caves. The torches jounced and splashed the dark with light.

Peculiar contraptions were being trundled along. I saw wheels and – wings. As the crowd swarmed round us, Nemian said, 'Claidi, I really need to ask you about—' But then we were being swarmed on along the flat table of stone.

'Ask away,' I shouted.

'It's all right,' he shouted back. 'It'll have to wait. There's this thing they do here. The chief told me. They fly.'

'Oh, I see.'

Of course I didn't. And besides, all this seemed irrelevant, after the sky, and my mother's dusk-sky name.

When everyone bundled to a sort of halt, I idly watched about six of the Featherers being strapped into the wheeled and winged structures.

There was a kind of seat, and pedals to move the wheels. Their arms were fitted into the wings, which were made of wood, I thought, and covered, like my gown, with feathers. It all looked absurd.

The crowd was calling out a single phrase over and over again, everyone dead drunk and grinning ear to ear, and the men on the winged things raised and lowered the wings with a dry creaking sound.

'What are they calling?' I said to Nemian, not really caring.

'Well, Claidi, you see they pedal over the cliff here, and then they flap their wings.'

'Oh. Sounds daft to me.'

'In a way. It's a festival to honour their god.'

'You mean God?'

'Not quite.'

'If they go – over the cliff? – then isn't that dangerous?'

'Exceedingly. The flying action somewhat lessens the fall. But they usually break an arm or a leg. That's what they're shouting, *Break a leg*! It means good luck.'

My mouth, trained to it by now, fell open on a reflex.

The pedallers were off anyway, thundering forward along the flat, arms and wings already vigorously waving.

And each one came to the edge, the edge of white cliff and diamond-dazzled night – space – and *rolled off*.

Everyone else, also Nemian and I, ran to the edge and peered after them.

There they went, down and down. In the air, they flailed, flapping and spinning, grotesque and funny, and frightful.

And one by one, they hit the ground far below, each with a crash and a scream. Clouds of what looked like steam came foaming up.

The Featherers were cheering. I was so frightened to see, I couldn't look away.

But one by one all the men crawled from the shambles of their flying-machines, which were all in bits now.

'Only two broken arms, apparently,' said Nemian, turning from the GFO, who was burping and guffawing next to us. 'They take all year to build

110

their craft, and one minute to smash them. You can see, though, Claidi, it's a dust-pit down there. Like the wings, that helps cushion the fall.'

I was going to reply with something witty or just pathetic, when I found all the villagers were touching me again. Some had hold of my arms. They were tugging and hoisting, lifting me off my feet.

At last I lashed out. It wasn't any good.

'Nemian – make them *stop*—'

Nemian looked startled. He said something in their awful language, and then turned and said it to the GFO.

But the GFO just gobbled and slapped Nemian on the back, and offered him the jar of drink again.

From Nemian's face I finally realized what was meant to happen now.

Whether they thought it wouldn't hurt, that I'd only *break a leg*, I didn't know. Or whether I was the best sacrifice to hand, a strayed traveller there exactly on the right night of the festival, I didn't know either.

Whatever it was, wingless in my feather dress, I was about to be slung over the cliff.

I screamed and kicked. I think I managed to ram my feet into someone's stomach. But it wasn't much of an achievement really. It wouldn't help.

And Nemian had been grabbed now, and was on the ground. I couldn't see him through their great stomping unbroken-unfortunately legs.

My bag – with this book – dropped back on the ground. I lost sight of it.

I was screeching and wailing. (You'll understand.)

And then, through all the din, the blur of panic and fear, a kind of dark explosion tore, and all at once I was flying – not off the cliff – but through the air, until I hit the ground which was only the flat hilltop, and then someone hauled me up and I landed on something both harder and softer—

Inexplicable. I kicked again and the something caught my foot.

'Here, you morbof, don't kick my okking eye out.'

Like surfacing from a depth of water, I rose and snarled into an unknown face. And yet, not the face of a Featherer. He was black as ebony, and he laughed even as he prevented me from clawing at his left eye.

'Watch it, chura. I'm here to *save* you.'

His hair was long, in tight braids, about ninety of them. How magnificent. But I didn't care. I tried to rip them out. Then he got my hands. He said, and he was running now, carrying me with him somehow, 'Look, chura, you're all right. We're going downhill, not off the cliff.'

It was true.

'My name isn't Chura.'

He looked vague but unconcerned.

112

'No,' he said, 'the Sheepers said you were Claadibaa.'

'*Claidi*.'

He laughed again. 'Fine. Claidi. You don't know, do you? *Chura* only means "darling".'

We arrived where? It was a hillside.

Up there, torch flash, howls, cries, the rasp of metal clashing and a sharp bang, the noise of shot, a gun.

'Nemian—' I cried – 'my *book*—'

'Book's here, Claidi,' said this fantastic being who I'd tried to disfigure. 'Nemian? *That* him? He's all right.'

He handed me this book. Not the sack. That was gone. Didn't matter. I clasped the book, and I sobbed. Sorry, but I did. Only once or twice.

My rescuer kindly patted me. 'Everything's all right.'

Apparently everything was all right.

'They were going to throw me over,' I unnecessarily reminisced.

He said, 'Drink this.' I pushed it away, but it was pushed back, and it was only absolutely delicious water. As I gulped, he said, 'We had to wait, you see. Be sure. Make certain we hadn't got the wrong end of the stick. So we followed you up, hung round the Feather village. Argul said, let them – the Tribe, that is – get drunk, make it easier, seeing we were a bit out numbered. He ran straight in to get you just then, only he was sort of detained – a

113

couple of blokes with knives. So I had the lucky pleasure of getting you away. I'm Blurn.'

You'll think I'm dotty. I instantly remembered the shouts at the Sheeper guest-house: *Kill it properly, Blurn. Don't eat it alive.*

Somehow I kept quiet. He'd saved me. There are limits.

Men were streaming down the hill. All bandits. Oh well.

Argul stood by the spot where they'd planted one torch left over from the Throwing-Claidi-off-the-Cliff Festival.

He stared at me, his dark eyes much darker than night. And not so friendly. (Blurn had told me Argul's name. I think I already knew, and that he was their leader.)

'Thanks,' I said to Argul. But that was mean. I added, 'I owe you my life.' Just what I'd thought Nemian ought to say.

But Nemian was over in a wagon, lying down, rather the worse for wear.

Argul nodded coldly.

'Don't mention it. We went out of our way. But I'm sure you two can pay us back for our efforts.'

With what? I glared at him. 'Do you only help people in order to get a reward?'

Some of them laughed. I realized at once, only at my cheek.

Argul glanced round anyway and they stopped.

He looked back at me.

'No, Miss Nuisance, I don't. I wouldn't normally bother.'

I'd been scared of him, but honestly, nearly being thrown to my death had made me a little braver. For the moment.

'I'm so glad,' I said sarcastically.

'See if it lasts,' said Argul.

He was the Grand Leader of the Mighty Bandits(!) He'd leaned on the Sheeper chariot, and gazed at that glass charm, and mocked us for not being worth robbing. And all the time waiting to see if I was, as the Sheepers must have let slip, the chosen Feather sacrifice. Making sure it was true, following, watching, seeing if he'd really have to bother to rescue me.

I felt angry and silly in that feather-itch dress. I felt alone. But one always is, I suppose.

THE BANDIT CAMP
ON THE MOVE

Until morning, we waited in the hills. They'd made a camp there, the five bandits. They'd come on ahead, and all the rest had to catch up.

All night they came riding in, on horses, with wagons, and dogs, these very well trained, alert and glossy and quiet.

In the increasingly enormous camp, there was

115

one big central fire. They sat round it. Unlike the dogs, they made a lot of noise, just as I remembered.

The Featherers had fled. Probably not all of them, judging from the sounds of knives and rifles I'd heard.

Blurn had told me, matter-of-factly, the Sheepers had sold us – me – to the Featherers. I was *barter*. Worse, the Sheepers had actually been out raiding to catch a girl sacrifice for the Featherers. No wonder they didn't mind taking Nemian and me to their town. (I recall the welcome, the drums, whistles and poppies.)

I feel awful about this. I'd rather liked the Sheepers. They seemed innocent – and kind.

The bandits of course seemed horrifying, and they were the ones who rescued me.

Obviously they too have a (probably sinister) reason for this. I must be on my guard. I've learnt the hard way not to trust anyone out here. One always learns the hard way. Is there any other?

During the night I went to see Nemian. There are bandit women, too, and one had given me bandit girl's clothes – trousers, tunic, even some bracelets with *gold coins* hanging from them, and coin earrings! I was touched, but I think all the women look like that here, and it was as automatic on her part to give me ornaments as to provide me with covering.

Nemian was sitting on some rugs in one of

the bandit wagons. He didn't recognize me, just glanced up and said, 'I'd appreciate some more beer, if you can spare it.'

'*More* beer? You'll burst,' I said, annoyed.

He flicked me his *look* then. Smiled.

'Claidi. I always know it's you by your gentle manner.'

Someone had apparently kicked him in the ribs though. And there was a purple bruise on his cheek. (Is he accident prone? No that's unfair. He'd been trying to stop them throwing me off the cliff. He hadn't been able to, but that wasn't his fault.)

A girl came in with the beer anyway, without being asked. He was so lovely to her, I was jealous, and left the wagon. (He seemed to have forgotten he'd wanted to question me about not knowing the name of my mother.)

Apparently I'm bad-tempered and jealous. A pretty awful person. I never knew this before. But then, I was never in love before. Am I? In love? I don't know what I am. Or who.

Argul, the leader, had gone into a tent and was soon joined by his second-in-command, who is Blurn.

I saw the bandit who'd whooped and caught the knife in his teeth. He's called Mehmed. Everytime he sees *me*, he *laughs*.

I'm not sure I'm so pleased to be here, really.

Finally I went to the wagon another woman said I could sleep in, and when I woke up, we were travelling. The wagon was still empty apart from me. I'd thought I'd have to share it.

I put my head out, and we were coming down from the hills, into yet another dusty desert. It looked so dreary. I tried to write a bit of this, and gave up because of the bumpy ride.

After that, I admired the paintings on the high leather roof, and thought how Blurn had told me the wagons are old, but in good repair since always cared for. He said each family had one, and passed it on. The horses and dogs are mostly the same, these ones descendants of others from centuries ago. Blurn said, to the bandits, the word *Hulta*, which is *a camp*, means also *Family*. To be part of the bandit camp is to be part of the bandit family. But it's a family always on the move.

I feel insulted, as if I've been made a fool of, but I'm not sure why. I found out, you see, the wagon I've been travelling in is Argul's own.

There were of course chests in it and pieces of wagon furniture, rugs and stools and jars. There were even some books I found – yes, I was nosing about, but not much – I recognized the language in only two of them. I'd also noticed knives and scabbards and shirts and boots and things lying around in corners. This morning I said, to make conversation with the bandit woman who came by with some food, 'Where are the others who live in this wagon?' And she said, 'It's Argul's wagon.'

She did add that he rides a horse by day and prefers the tent at night, and only uses the wagon now and then, but I felt immensely uncomfortable, as if he'd played a joke on me. Also in some way labelled me as a possession. I can't think why he would want me. Does he imagine I'm valuable? That must be it. Nemian has said something. I'm a princess from a House. So it's threatening as well.

Naturally I got out instantly.

Nemian was elegantly riding a horse by now, talking to the bandits as if they're old friends. He does seem to love being with new people. Is this a nice quality or rather shallow of him? And does it mean he has lost interest totally in me because I'm not *new* any more? Doubtless.

Then Blurn appeared and said there was a mule to ride, for me.

Only after I'd managed to get on to the mule – nearly fell off both sides twice – did I think to demand, 'Is this mule *Argul's*?'

'Nope,' said Blurn, 'my aunt's.'

'Then doesn't your aunt—'

'She's got plenty more,' said Blurn, as if we were discussing pairs of slippers.

The mule is a pain.

It's got an adorable face and wonderful eyelashes, but it kicks out at things, and *wriggles*. Nemian says a mule doesn't wriggle. It does, it does. I've tried to feed it and groom it to show it I'm worthwhile and it ought to like me. But it takes no notice, just tries

119

to kick me as I turn my back, and then wriggles as I try to swing gracefully into its saddle.

Needless to say, passing bandits, men and women both, find this exquisite fun.

'There goes Claidi-baa again,' they say, as I plummet off in the dust. And that's another thing. They keep calling me by a Sheeper version of my name. After what the Sheepers did, I find that extra aggravating.

Tonight there was a Hulta council.

We all gathered about the huge central fire, from which the cook-pots had been removed, though some vegetables and loaves went on baking in the hot ashes.

Argul strode out of his tent. He looked – astonishing.

I mean, he did look the way a leader should. A young king. Polished black hair and eyes, tall and lean and tawny. He was covered in gold fringes and coins, and silver rings and things. Barbaric, I'm sure the House would have said. A 'barbarian'. Nemian was smiling a little. But then, one of the prettiest bandit girls was sitting next to Nemian, as she always seems to be now.

The council was because we were all going to Peshamba. The bandits hadn't been there before, or not for generations, although they knew of the city. (At first I'd been confused and thought Peshamba was Nemian's city, but it isn't. I'd thought *all* cities had crumbled or been blown over. Wrong, obviously.) (The House told so many lies to us. Or else the House was extremely ignorant. Both?)

Anyway, the route to Peshamba is long and passes through this dust desert, or there's another way, across something called the Rain Gardens. The council was to decide, by vote, which way we go.

I'm impressed, but sceptical. If Argul is leader, doesn't he ever lead? What's the point of having a leader if everyone has a hand in every decision?

(Blurn said they'd voted on rescuing me. I assumed they must all have been in favour, but apparently only half had. Now when I talk to them, I wonder which ones didn't think I was worth the trouble. I don't blame them. But yuk. In the end only five bandits went after the Featherers.)

I didn't have the nerve to say to Blurn, Why *did* Argul bother? Afraid of what the answer will be. Oh, we're going to sell you as a mule acrobat in Peshamba or something.

They talked about the Rain Gardens. It was vague. None of them are sure quite what happens there, although travellers tend to avoid the place. It does rain.

Personally, anything rather than this dust bowl.

But I didn't get a vote, nor Nemian.

He didn't seem put out. Princes are above such things? I'm only a pretend princess, aren't I. Or was it less interesting than the bandit girl combing his hair? Hmm.

121

The vote was for the Gardens.

Afterwards, the bandits sat on, drinking. Some of them talked and played with their dogs. Several had stolen female dogs from the Featherer village. I was really glad, because already these dogs are being cared for and looking healthier and more calm.

This in mind, I went to see my mule. Also so as not to have to look at Nemian as the girl plaited blue beads into his golden lion's mane. Come on, Nemian. That's what the Sheepers did with the sheep.

The mule of course wasn't pleased to see me.

I stood over it, rubbing its nose – it does have a nice nose – and offering it some mule food.

'It's Claidi,' I said firmly. 'Dear Claidi that you know and love. Giving you a delicious snack you don't deserve.'

'You expect too much of it,' said someone. 'With a horse, you'd have a better chance.'

It wasn't Blurn, who I half-way trust – must remember I mustn't – so I turned.

There stood Argul the Bandit Leader, gleaming from the distant fire and lamps at his back, as if rimmed in gold.

What should I do? Grovel because I owe him my life? Or be rude because I know I'm being used?

You'll have guessed.

'Well since I don't have a horse, that's such a help, isn't it.'

'I'm surprised you haven't taken one,' said Argul. 'Just bite someone's nose off and steal his mount. Why not.'

'You're the practised bandits, not me.'

'You could learn.'

I thought, I'm Princess Claidissa Star. My mother was called Twilight Star. I raised my head.

'Why did you save my life?'

'Why did I.'

Inside my raised head I thought, *Yes, and I spent my days as a slave.*

I looked down.

Argul said, 'You can have a horse instead of a mule. Starting to ride will be uncomfortable at your age, but it'll be worth it. Want to try?'

Seeing me slipping and rolling off the mule wasn't fun enough. Off a horse might really be a laugh.

'No, thank you.'

'Tronking hell,' said Argul.

He turned his back and strode away. His hair swung like a wave. The cloak swung, and gold discs chimed on it. Musical.

I wish I'd said yes. And what did he mean, my *Age*, as if I was thirty or something.

A long time has gone by since I wrote that. A lot's been happening. In all kinds of ways.

Something needs to be said about the bandits and the Hulta.

It's awkward.

The House depended on life being carved in stone, and the rules of life were iron. You couldn't make changes. You couldn't change your mind about anything important.

But I think life isn't about that. It's *about* changing. If you grow, you change, don't you. A kid becomes an adult. A puppy becomes a dog. You can't stay still and you can't stay always thinking one thing only, especially when you see it wasn't right. It was a mistake.

But you know all this. I bet you do.

It's just – I didn't. Or did I?

First of all, I have to describe a morning, still in the floury desert, and me coming along to the fire, and there's Blurn, stuffing himself with the nut porridge the bandits often have. And Mehmed, the knife-thrower, yells, 'Kill it, Blurn!' And another man, Ro, shouts, 'Make sure it's dead!'

And Claidi stands there, seeing for the first, that what she heard through a window wasn't something horrible, but just a *joke*.

They were joking about Blurn's method of eating. And then Blurn turned and made other appalling comments on Mehmed and Ro's methods of eating (which, admittedly, are worse).

So, you don't always learn the hard way. You can learn a silly, funny way.

Which, too, is another lesson.

I'm getting tangled up.

For example. Since leaving A's wagon, I've slept each night in the open on a pillow with a blanket, supplied me by the woman who'd come by with the food.

She must have seen I was nervous.

She said, 'There aren't many insects here.' Then, noting I was still unnerved, 'No lions. But if they come around, the look-out will know.' *Then*, seeing me *still* worried, she added, 'If you don't want a man friend, no one will disturb you.' '*Oh*, yes,' I said. She looked me up and down and said, 'Where you come from must have been a bad place. People don't creep up on people here. We're not leopards. If you like someone, tell him. If not, you can be private.'

Did I believe her? No.

I was panicky and couldn't sleep.

I *had* a man friend. I had Nemian.

Correction. I hadn't got a man friend. Or a friend?

In the House, people had fallen for each other. (Never me.) But you had to be so careful. (My parents, for instance. Exiled for being in love and having a child.)

One heard such stories about the Waste. And *bandits*—

They're all right. No one intrudes.

Probably they just don't notice me. I'm so bad-tempered, boring, jealous, tacky.

I saw Nemian one evening, one *twilight*, talking to the bandit girl. They were gazing into each other's eyes. I felt a sort of pain, sharp and cold–hot. I slunk off.

Next day, a horse arrived. Blurn brought it.

Can't help this. I like Blurn. It isn't just that he rescued me, he's just – I just *like* him. And he's with Argul a lot. So . . . I don't know. Somehow it helps. (Blurn, by the way, has a girlfriend. She's terrific. Anyway I don't mean I like Blurn *that* way.)

The horse. Let me tell you about the horse. It was blue-black – like the sky that night. And it had thinking black eyes. It stood there, thoughtful and beautiful, its silk tail swishing faintly, and Blurn said, 'He says, for you.'

'Who says?' As if I didn't know.

'Him. Argul. This is a female horse, a mare. She's bred down from—' couldn't follow – 'something of something-something line. She can run like the wind, but she's gentle as honey.'

Naturally I was about to refuse, but the horse, the mare, made a soft noise down her nose. I went up to her and stroked her face.

'Not scared, are you,' approved Blurn.

'She's wonderful.'

'Hey, Claidi,' said Blurn. He gave me his huge white smile. I felt happy. I'd done something right. At last.

And the horse – she's called Sirree – is a dream.

126

She's so patient with me. You can tell she knows I'm learning, finding out. But when I feed her or talk to her, she *listens*. Absolute agony, though. I might as well be thirty. The bandit woman – she also has a name, Teil – explained that it will be awful for a while. Your body has to get used to getting into, and holding, this position. It isn't too bad during the day. But when I totter off, and in the morning – Ow! Ow! Ow!

Don't care.

That mule gave me a look. Blurn said mules always do. They have Mule Ideas. But horses understand people, as dogs and wolves do, and often cats and birds.

Then we came across some travellers in the desert.

In a valley, about five, low-slung carts, and some *thing* under lots of sacks, being pulled by dogs.

When Argul's outriders spotted this, and we (me) heard and rode along the line of wagons to see, I thought, Oh, now A's bandits will tear down and rob and murder everyone.

However, the bandits just went down and helped put a wheel back on one of the carts.

The dog teams were in fine tail-wagging condition. The bandits laughed and mucked about among the other travellers. Sounds of this jollity drifted up the valley.

They came to supper.

Speech was a problem. Hardly anyone spoke their language. Argul did a bit.

Among the sacks they had a big stone statue. They were taking it somewhere, for some reason.

No one was robbed.

Argul *gave* them supplies, bread and dried oranges, rice and beer.

The Hulta do rob people. They came after Nemian and me and the Sheeper, and wanted money. (Although A said he couldn't use it and gave it back. And they were following us to see if I was going to be sacrificed . . .) They *do* kill people. Unless they just frightened the Featherers off.

Dawn broke, and the travellers went away with their statue, which was of a huge bear. (Blurn said it was a bear.)

Under the pink sky, we all saw a wash of land sweeping up and up, and beyond, something was giving off fumes, pushing redness into the pink.

'Gardens,' said Mehmed. (Did I say, Mehmed's really all right too?)

I've lost touch with Nemian. He hasn't been anywhere near where I am.

'The Rain Gardens?' I inquired.

'Yup.'

We stared at red melting in pink.

It's unknown, to me, to Nemian, and to the Hulta.

Just like life. No one knows what's round the next bend, over the next hill. It could be heaven-on-earth or death. We can only go on, and find out.

Nemian appeared at this moment. He rode up on his smart horse, and the bandit girl was on a horse beside him.

He shot me a loving smile.

I glared.

'Ah – Claidi . . . how are you?'

'I haven't thought about it. How do I seem?'

'Fantastic,' enthused my absent-now-present-'friend'. 'We must talk,' said Nemian.

'Oh, talk.'

'Save it,' said Mehmed. 'We have to get through *there* first.'

Just then soft rain began to fall. It was pale, yet it smelled sooty, like old fires.

Nemian's hair was flattened. Dark gold. Something hurt in me, and worse when the bandit girl, whose name I don't even know, handed him her scarf to wipe his face.

As they rode off, he sent back a stare that seemed full of yearning, as if it was me he wanted to be with. As I say, as he rode off.

I can't trust Nemian either, and I never could.

So on over the next hill, round the next bend.

I decided to go back to the wagon to write this.

All right, Argul's wagon – but he'd be out there in the rain, planning, and if he turned up here I'd be off like a shot. And I'd only borrowed Sirree. A borrowed friend's better than none. I could feel my face getting very long.

When I was outside again, Mehmed said vaguely, 'Still wondering which half of us didn't want to rescue you?'

My head jerked up. He grinned at my defiance.

'You're a bit slow, Claidibaari.'

'*Thank* you.'

'It was a *joke*, Claidi.'

I wanted to hit his dark face. Was too sensible to do so.

Mehmed said, 'I *told* Blurn you'd believe it, take it to heart, get all miserable. We didn't *vote*, Claidibaabaa. There wasn't time, anyway. When Argul found out, he just picked four of us who weren't doing anything, and we rode after you. He is *leader*, you duppy girl.'

NIGHTMARES BY DAY

Once you're really soaked, probably it doesn't matter being in the rain.

So that's all right.

Everyone looks half drowned.

Even inside the wagons it doesn't stay dry,

130

because crawling in and out of them, the rain rubs off.

The rain is red.

That is, it looks red, and stains reddish.

Teil brought me a piece of treated leather to wrap this book in, to protect the pages. She said, wasn't this a long letter. She thinks it's a letter. Is it? Maybe. She also told me the bandits have a store of ink pencils, so if this one runs out, that will be handy.

I'm not in A's wagon now. In this weather, I assume he's using it. I share one with some of the girls. I may be beginning to follow some of the bandits' language, too. They have two languages really, the one I speak, and this other one mixed in it.

At night, as the red rain drives on the roof, we suck sticks of treacle-candy, and they tell stories. I told one, as well. I made it up as I went along, but sort of pinched bits from my memory of House books. They seemed to like it, but theirs are better. I think theirs are true.

No one likes this place at all.

There are rocks and stones, some of them hundreds of *man-heights* high, as the bandits say. Either they've been shaped by the weather, or people carved them long ago. There are arches, walls, columns, towers with openings, and peculiar stairways, partly steps and partly slopes. It could almost be another ruin of some great city, not fallen but *melted*, like old candles.

On the horizon, on either side, to which the stone shapes stretch, about a mile or so away, are craters, out of which smokes sift and sometimes bubbles of crimson fire.

From some of these smoke-holes pillars of smoulder rise into the sky, which is always cloudy and tinged like a blush.

The smokes, the cindery heat and sudden flares of fire, seem to set the rain off overhead.

When it comes down, which it's always doing, it's like *wet* fire.

Why do they call this place Rain *Gardens*???

Last night one of the bandit girls, who's only a kid really, about seven, but she's just like a woman, striding about with a knife in her belt, and fierce as anything, told us a story of the Rain Gardens. She said the earth burst open, and fire rushed out and over, and smothered everything here. She said the ground we're riding and walking over is made of powdered and then cemented human bones.

Word goes it'll take seven or ten days to get through. We've been in for five so far. It's a bad dream, this.

Eleventh day, and no sign of the end. Argul rode round again, chatting to everyone. He was very cool. Blurn sat his horse, looking proud to have Argul for a leader. Even the older men listen to what Argul says. His father was the Hulta leader

132

before him, and his mother was also very powerful. She was a herbalist and, they say, even skilled with chemicals. A magician.

'Did you see that charm he wears round his neck?' asked Teil. 'His mother gave him that.'

I thought he was lucky to have known his mother. If that seems selfish, it is. I wish, how I wish, I'd known mine.

Then Teil said, 'She died when he was a child.' As if she'd read my mind, and was putting me right.

Today, from a rise, we could see where this ends, some miles off still. But the new region doesn't look very promising.

Peshamba is this way. Somewhere south.

What's first is apparently covered with some sort of vegetation. It looks thick and murky.

From books, I know lava and sulphur will nourish the soil once they've settled, and this vegetable area must be the result.

Everything *tastes* of soot and frequently smells of eggs that have gone off.

Sirree is damp, and streaked with red, no matter how I rub and groom her.

In the middle of last night we heard a weird sound.

It was a sort of booming *scream*.

The bandit girls and I pelted out of the wagon

133

with our hair on end. Everyone else was doing the same. All the usually quiet dogs were barking and yapping and the horses trampling at their pickets.

It went on and on – then stopped.

We were all saying What is it? What is it? And children were crying with fear. It was like a nightmare that had woken up with us all.

About two miles off to the left, a particularly vivid volcanic crater then started puffing up wine-red streams.

People began to say to each other, the noise had come from a lava vent. The gasses build up there and can make strange sounds, before the lava bursts out.

We hung around in the rain for ages, afraid the dire noise would start again. But it didn't.

Thought I would never sleep. But I did.

By the way, I haven't seen Nemian for days and nights. If I still suspected the bandits as much as I did, and perhaps still should, I'd think they had, as they say in the Hulta, *Put out his light*.

One of the girls though told me he keeps to a wagon, with the family of the girl he's taken up with.

He wouldn't like the wet, I suppose. And I'm sure they fuss over him. 'Ooh, can we get you another cushion, Nemian? Another slice of cake?'

Sometimes, when I think of it, I feel white-hot

anger. And bitter, too. Oddly, I *don't* think of him all that much. Am I the shallow one?

The land was like cracked paving, huge slabs, and behind us lay the wet red smoke, and before us lay a shadow.

Nemian rode through the last rain, until his horse, blonde and sleek, was walking by Sirree through the damp hot weirdness.

'Hallo, Claidi.'

'Hi.'

'You look and sound like a true bandit lady.'

I didn't reply.

Nemian said, 'What must you think of me?'

'Would you like a written answer? But it might cover several pages.'

'Perhaps not. It's admirable the way you've fitted in here. A princess among thieves.'

'I'm not a princess,' I said.

Now he didn't speak.

Down and up the line of horses, wagons, mules and so on, rolled a rumble of wheels, calls, curses and clatter, this now-familiar music.

'On the Princess Claidi thing, Jizania lied,' I said. Though I wasn't sure I believed it.

'She would never do that,' said he.

'Wouldn't she? She was going to have to. Otherwise they'd know she let you escape.'

'I see. That's observant. Clever. You are, aren't you, Claidi? Claidi, you're a jewel.'

'Yum,' I said.

I wouldn't look at him.

If I looked, I'd see. I'd lose my lofty tone. I'd start thinking he was really something all over again.

'Claidi, you've fitted in, and so have I, here. I'm also good at that. It's the way to get by. To survive. Don't judge me, Claidi. When we get to the next city, we *must* talk. I need to tell you things.'

'Fine.'

Ahead, someone called out. We were coming to the vegetation. The shadow.

'Claidi,' said Nemian, low and strong, his voice magically throbbing, 'I *need* you. Please, remember that.'

He was gone.

And we'd reached the—

The—?

Thinking later, I wondered if it's called Rain *Gardens* for this part. It is a kind of . . . garden. A wood, an orchard, of a sort.

Meadows of a sort came first. They had dark moss, and clumps of things that were 'flowering' – whippy dark leaves, pods like grey-pinkish bells. And mushrooms, striped black and yellow – they looked as poisonous as wasps.

In the 'meadows' there were 'trees'. The 'trees' became thicker and drew together and we rode into the garden–orchard–wood.

Well, the trees had trunks, veined and gnarled,

and roped over with ivies and creeper. But you could see through these trunks, they were semi-transparent – like enormous stems. And in the branches, where the creepers and ivies weren't, were blade-like leaves, a pale luminous green. And fruits.

Actually, the fruits were the oddest of all. The House Garden grew all kinds of fruit and vegetables in special plots and glass-houses. I'd never seen anything like this.

They were most like carrots, but carrots that had gone mad, twisting and turning, some of them curled up almost in a circle.

In those stories I'd now and then read in the library at the House, (hiding behind book stacks, generally found and beaten) any travellers who find unusually strange fruit, always eat it, and get ill. None of the bandits touched the fruit. Even the children didn't.

They must have known not to.

So neither did I. So neither can I offer an educational insight into what the fruits tasted like, or their effect.

The other bad side to all this is, of course, that this is exactly the kind of bad place the Waste is supposed to be filled with, according to the House. They'd been right.

And the trees dripped. Another sort of rain. Some sticky juice or resin. It didn't seem dangerous, didn't burn or sting, but it was soon all over everything, including clothes and hair. I felt as if I'd fallen into jam.

The tree-things rose up and up. Some were as tall as towers, tall as the trees in the Garden. It was dark, the overcast smoky sky mostly shut out.

The Hulta wagons seemed to move more quietly. The vegetation muffled sound, but also very little noise was being made. No calls or swearing. No kids running about. When the horses shook their bridles, which have bells and coins on them, the tinkling sounded flat, but also I saw riders putting out their hands to stop the bells jingling.

I said, Nemian had ridden off. I clucked to Sirree, and we went up the line of wagons, and Ro and Mehmed were there, riding along.

'It goes on for miles,' said Ro.

I hadn't asked. Everyone was probably asking everyone: How long does this bit last?

'Like it?' Mehmed asked me.

'Not a lot.'

'Gives me the creeps,' said Ro. 'Like that forest over north, remember, Mehm?'

'The one with panthers?' inquired Mehmed.

'Yeah, and those trees that lean over and grab you and wind you up in stuff so you can't move, and then slowly digest you over months.'

'Oh,' said Mehmed.

They looked greenish. But we all probably did from the green-black shadows.

A carrot fruit fell off a tree and landed on the ground, where it burst in a repulsive way.

We were looking at this, when another shower of carrots came down, all bursting. And then the vegetable wood was *shaking*.

Long dull thuds seemed to come up from the ground, out of the air.

'An earthquake,' Ro decided.

The branches overhead also shook furiously. Creepers snapped and uncoiled, falling like ropes. The air was full of wiry stems, and leaves, and horrible bursting fruit.

There was already shouting, but now there were yells, shrieks.

Through the depths of the wood came a terrifying crackling *rush*. It was like a wind blowing, but a wind that was solid.

'Something's coming!' yelled Mehmed.

It was. People were calling in panic, 'Where is it?' And 'Over there! It's there!' or 'No, that way—' And then one voice cried out in a ragged howl, 'No – up there! It's *above*!'

And so we all looked up, and from high up in the trees, the face of a *demon* looked back at us.

My heart stopped. Or it felt like it.

That face—

It was yellowish, a mask, with large black eyes and pointed tusks – it had a mane of darkness that somehow flashed with golden fires—

And from the mouth there burst an impossible ear-shattering thunder that was a *scream*.

The horses reared. Sirree reared. I don't know why I didn't fall off. Ro did. Dogs howled. Then somehow, silence.

Dogs flattened on their bellies. Horses shivering. The rest of us turned to stone. Staring, beyond terror almost. (And a glimpse of Argul I only recalled after, somehow up at the front, confronting the menace, between all of us, and it—)

While the thing in the trees stared *down* at us.

It was like the bear-statue, only not. It had long arms, incredibly long, hanging now loosely over the limb of the tree where it squatted. Its claws were the length of my arm, or so they looked. I think it was altogether about twice the height of a man.

It was covered in fur, black fur, streaked with what looked like rust. But also the fur was full of creepers and ivy, like the trees, and with other growths, savage flowers, funguses – and there were smaller things living in the fur and the growths – mice, maybe, snakes – all weaving in and out, so tiny eyes sparkled and were gone, and sinuous little bodies moved like fish in a pool.

Round its head, its insane face, whirled this golden crown that spun. For the crown was several enormous flies, golden and green, constant companions to the demon bear-thing, must be, for it took no notice of them, as it took no notice of all the creatures living on it.

It was a *world*.

That awful face stared down. You know, it was a wise face, too, but not wise in any way I'd ever understand or want to.

The jaws stretched, and again out came that appalling ear-splitting roar-scream.

None of us now made a sound.

The beast hung over us, still, yet also in endless total motion, from the movement of its companion life.

But then it grew bored with us. It raised one long, long arm, dripping with hair and leaves and mice, and the great gold flies, each the size, I'd say, of one of Ro's huge feet, whirled in a joyful dance. And smoke poured from its fur – dust, I think, from the lava pits.

The beast plucked a handful of the fruits, and put them in its mouth.

Then flinging up both arms now, in clouds of leaves and smoke, it sprang high, high across the boughs, caught some distant tree limb, and swung away into the shadow of the wood.

No one moved or spoke for about an hour.

'An ape,' said Ro.

'Bear,' Mehmed.

'Ape, stupid. Bears don't swing through the trees.'

I began to hear whispering, and then some loud

141

joking all around. Argul was talking to some men and women, glancing our way a lot, no doubt to see what M and R were doing.

We were alive. Shakily I stroked Sirree.

The House had been right again. There are monsters in the waste. This one, luckily, was a vegetarian.

PESHAMBA

After all that, Peshamba was a relief.

Also a shock.

Peshamba is beautiful.

In fact, getting through the rest of the monster wood, wondering off and on if there'd be any more of the bear-apes, these more hungry and less fussy ones, or worse things than bear-apes (?!!) only took the rest of the day.

We came out of the wood before the sun set. This in itself was a relief, and I heard some 'prayers' spoken, sort of chants to do with thanks. (I'm still puzzled about this God-gods thing. I must ask somebody sensible. There were no gods, prayers or shrines in the House. No idea like this at all. Or none I ever heard.)

Beyond the wood there was a grassy plain. It started as dry, burnt-looking grass, but then unrolled into greenness, and then *rainbows*.

As the sun went down I stood up on a rise, and

the distance was emerald, with films of mauve and blue and rose.

'Wild flowers,' said the seven-year-old with the knife, (she's *called* Dagger).

'Oh,' I said.

Now what should I think? The House said monsters and deserts and criminals. Spot on. But the House said too that only the House and the Garden had greenness and flowers.

Jizania hadn't though. But I don't somehow trust Jizania, now.

'You've been here before?' I asked Dagger.

'No. We don't normally travel in this direction. Best trade is north and east.'

She must mean the best places to rob.

Politely I didn't say this.

'You've seen lots of wild flowers,' I said.

'Seen about everything,' boasted Dagger.

Could be true for all I know.

That night, grasshoppers sang on the plain.

In the morning the Hulta rambled on. We rode across the green grass with the flowers. They were something, all right. Wild hyacinths, wild roses, drifts of convolvulus and lilies. Wonderful scent. Looking back, the shadow wood just slid away.

Then the city started to be visible ahead.

I didn't believe my eyes. It was like jewellery.

But as it got nearer and nearer, it got better and better.

The pale walls cascading up were topped with

gold. (It isn't quite. It's thin gold–leaf, but even so.) Windows glittered like sweets because they had colours in them. And there were domes. White and lucent as lamps with a faint candle inside. And ruby, and turquoise blue, with gold patterns all over.

The bandits were also impressed, but they had heard of Peshamba.

I wondered what Nemian thought. According to the little he'd said, his own city was tremendous, better than anywhere. Could it be better than here?

When you come close, the walls appear higher than five houses, piled one on another, and inside, other higher walls go up.

At the front, like a blue shining apron, is a lake. Peshamba seems to be standing in it, and partly is. The reflection of the city floats in the water, and Peshamba floats above, between water and sky.

'Is the water drinkable?' I asked Dagger. She shrugged. She does this when she doesn't know something, as if to say, 'If I don't, it can't be important.'

Anyway, when we reached the water, half the bandit men flung off their shirts, cloaks, jackets and decorations, and plunged in to swim. The women found a quieter part among some willows.

Was anyone watching from the walls? Did they think an invasion had arrived?

But later, when we went over the stone bridge

I forgot to mention stretched across the lake, a gate in the wall stood wide open.

Beyond was a narrow way, paved with marble. And on it stood a giant, half the height of a man again.

He was encased in a uniform made of metal, and in his hand there was a huge axe. His helmet was gold with a white plume. His face was entirely masked in gold.

I'd got up near the front of the Hulta horde, and I could see Argul sitting on his horse, looking in at the giant gravely.

Thinking of books again, I said to Mehmed, 'Does someone have to fight the giant?'

'Wouldn't fancy it much. He's one big tronker.'

Just then, the giant spoke.

'*Name yourselves.*'

The strangest voice. Perhaps the mask made it sound so peculiar.

Argul called out, 'The Hulta.'

'*Your business.*'

'Travellers,' said Argul. And lightly, 'Sightseers.'

The giant lowered his axe.

'*Do no harm in Peshamba, and Peshamba does no harm to you.*'

The Hulta consists of a mass of people. We squashed through, wagons and animals, the lot, and the giant stood aside in a kind of alcove in the marble wall.

Ro was there. 'Wouldn't fancy taking *him* on.'

145

Teil pushed up, carrying one of the little girls astride her horse. (The Hulta children can ride at four or five. Hence Argul's comment on my great age.)

'I've heard of this,' said Teil, waving at the giant. 'It's clockwork.'

Ro snorted. He went up to the giant. 'Here, mate. You a *doll*?'

The gold mask creaked down to Ro. It wasn't a mask. It was a gold-painted face made of metal, which gave no answer.

Ro backed off.

We went on, and where the narrow way ended, passed through another, wider gate.

Here were two long lines of guards, standing bolt upright. They had axes over their shoulders, wore scarlet, and were covered in braid, epaulets, spurs, spikes, metal plates. They weren't giants, however. Really not much taller than me.

As we went by, they presented arms, bringing their axe-hafts down on the ground with a bang.

'Are they crazy here?' I said.

Teil said, 'No. If someone attacks, these things go wild. And they can't be hurt, either, or stopped.'

I asked how she knew. 'Oh,' said Teil, 'word gets around.'

There were several more passages and gates, all with the clockwork doll-guards. Some even had rifles with silver set in the stocks. They certainly were better looking than the House Guards.

Eventually we all muddled into a huge garden – they call it here a *park*.

Blue cedars and olive-green palms stretched across the sky. Cypress trees carefully shaped to dark, waxed tassels. Fountains. A procession of snow-white ducks idled across a lawn.

Argul was riding down the line.

'If you don't know, be careful here.' He saw Ro peering greedily after the ducks. 'Watch it, Ro.' Argul pointed. High on a slim tower as pink as marshmallow, a glass thing was turning slowly round and round, flashing in the sun. 'They keep an eye on everything. See that? It's looking at us.'

'What, *that*?'

'That.'

The message went down the line of people and wagons.

Across the park, we could now see wonderfully dressed figures moving about, and girls in glimmering silks playing ball.

Blurn appeared.

'Watch it, Ro.'

'All right, all right.'

In the park was a large building with courtyards clustered around and inside it. It was burstingly full. It's named the Travellers' Rest.

I saw some new (to me) animals which someone told me are 'Zebras', not horses. They had black and white stripes that make you dizzy. And there were three teams of 'Oxen' the colour of walnuts.

147

Tents had been pitched, carts and wagons stood about, courtyards streamed with drying coloured washing. There were wells and pools, and ornamental fountains, all crowded.

Impossible racket. Sounded to me like a thousand different languages.

Going up some stairs carrying bundles, I saw, over a wall, more of the city lying below. There were the jewellery domes, and there a slim green tower with a golden bell in it, and squares, and roads, and buildings as decorated as cakes, and all pale glowing colours with sun on them. And gardens – everywhere gardens. (There was another of those turning, flashing crystals I could see, as well.)

Over the smells of Hulta and people and animals generally, scents of spice and cooking, and tobacco, of vines and flowers, and the smell of *brickwork* in the sun that I'd half forgotten.

We girls and women on our own got quite a big room to ourselves. Like all the other women in the Rest, we immediately began washing clothes and underthings and sheets, hanging them out of the windows, and even from the rafters.

The queue for the bathrooms was long, but worth it.

I'd forgotten too the delight of cool-skin-temperature water scented with a few stolen herbs and perfumes. Here you can *buy* them. Or I couldn't, but Teil did, and gave some to me.

148

And soap and other things to keep one smelling nice.

I washed my hair. The last time was in the red rain. (I'd gone to groom Sirree, but it had already been done. The Rest has its own grooms, and Argul had *paid* to have all the horses and dogs tended. Even a couple of Hulta pet monkeys were being brushed, and scented with banana essence.)

At first, the people of the city were hard for me to sort out from all the other people packed in here.

They seem a mixture, like everyone. But their clothes are always the most amazing silky stuff, and fabulous colours. So that's how I identify Peshambans now. Oh, and sometimes they wear masks. Not over the whole face, just the eyes. It's a fashion – to make them more like the dolls this city's supposed to be full of?

Excitement in the room we share. There's a festival tonight. (I thought of the Featherers and felt uneasy, but it's nothing like that.) Large chests from the wagons had been opened and astonishing garments taken out. Fit to rival Peshamban clothes.

One of the girls insisted on giving me – it was a 'present' – a deep blue dress sewn with embroidery and silver discs. Everyone clapped when I'd put it on. I felt shy, touched, and also rather resentful. A funny combination, but I think they feel sorry for

149

me about Nemian. (Who, I may add, someone told me has already gone swanning off into the city.)

I did like myself in the dress when I glanced into the mirror.

We made each other up, black round the eyes and powder, and scented sticks of colour for the mouth.

'Pretty Claidibaabaa!' they cried, prancing round me. I really *was* the centre of attention.

Someone else then gave me silver earrings with sapphires in them. Real true sapphires.

'*Hultai chura!*' they squealed.

I concluded that must mean Darling of the Hulta. (!!!) (But why?)

We had lunch in the main hall, where food can be *bought* – pancakes and vegetables – then later in the room they were teaching me steps to wild Hulta dances, gallops and stampings and tossing the head (like a horse).

I haven't laughed like this for so long. We laughed ourselves daft.

I feel a bit guilty now, thinking how Daisy and Pattoo and I found ways to giggle and mess around despite the filthy rules and cruelty of the House.

But the afternoon is turning over to sunfall and soon it'll be that time which is my mother's lovely name.

I can't help it. I want to have fun tonight.

Nemian – well. Grulps, as the ruder Hulta say. Yes, *grulps*.

Someone will like me, dance with me, hold my hand. I'm not going to worry about if or who. Someone *will*. It's that sort of night.

And I never was a princess. That was a lie. Wasn't it?

There's a song . . . it said . . . Moon in a cloud . . .

How to make sense of this.

I'll try, but please, please my unknown, invented friend, be patient, it's not easy.

A huge square in the last daylight, with tall gracious buildings around, views of parks, and cloudy dark-green trees, and down here orange trees with orange-gold fruits. At the east end of the square, some steps go up to a pavement of apricot marble. On this stands another high white tower. At the tower's top, a clock. Actually, a CLOCK.

It must be, if it had been down on the square and anyone could've measured it, about the size of the Alabaster Fish Pool in the Garden of the House. Vast.

The CLOCK is in a frame of gold and silver, and up there, in front of it, stood three carved figures, very lifelike, except for being so big, painted and gilded. One was a girl and one a man, and in the middle was a white horse up on its hind legs. Out of the horse's forehead ran a crystal horn. And later I noticed it also had silvery folded wings.

As we arrived, people were leaning out of small

151

windows at the tower top, and lighting hanging lamps.

The square was full, and a cheer went up from the Peshambans, and from everyone else. Even we cheered. I wasn't sure why, but it seemed polite.

Blurn appeared, very smart and over-the-top in dark red, patterned boots, and earrings.

'Hi, Claidi. Like the clock?'

'It's good.'

'They worship it,' said Blurn.

'Sorry?'

'The Peshambans. They worship that clock.'

The CLOCK was a . . . god?

But Blurn had stridden on. And as the soft lights spangled over the CLOCK, other lamps were lighting all around.

The sky got bluer, deeper. Twilight. Stars came out.

There were long tables laid with such pretty food, wonderful colours and designs, and fruits I'd never seen before. And there were glass jugs in ice of wine or juice or mixtures of both, shining like rubies and topaz and jade.

Dagger slipped through the crowd. She wore green and a Peshamban mask shaped like a dragonfly.

'It's all free,' she breathed. 'Cos of the festival.'

She grabbed a plate and piled it with food, far more than I've ever seen her eat, and darted off.

But by then the centre of the square was clearing.

There was to be dancing. Apparently all this tonight was done in the square, to honour the CLOCK.

One of the bandit girls, Toy, pulled me.

'Come on, Claidi.'

'But I can't dance.'

'Haven't we spent *hours* teaching you, Claidibaa?'

'But that was Hulta dances—' I feebly protested.

'There'll *be* Hulta dances. They play all dances for all the visitors. And we showed you three Peshamban dances too.' 'But—' 'Hulta have come here before, in the past, remember?'

I was sure now I *wouldn't* remember a step, would make a fool of myself.

But somewhere a band was tuning up, and I recognized for a second a phrase from a tune the girls had sung that afternoon in the Travellers' Rest.

I found myself in the square's centre in a line of laughing girls and women, between Teil and Toy.

A glance along the line made me feel happy, because everyone was shining and glittering and laughing. Peshamban girls with glass or real jewels sewn all over their clothes, and masks of cats and butterflies. Bandit girls clinking with coins. Women from all sorts of places I didn't know, hadn't ever known *existed*. At least I had Nemian to thank for *this*. For this freedom, this finding out. (Incidentally where was . . . ?)

You've guessed, haven't you. I was avoiding looking at the line of men opposite. It wasn't going to matter too much, this time. You changed partners three times in this particular dance.

Even so.

The band was over there, under that fringed awning. Stringed instruments and flutes, what looked like a cello, and two drums. And two silver sheets that were suddenly clashed together, and the dance had begun.

I looked up into the amused and rather (already) drunk face of Ro.

A surge of relief and disappointment.

Too late to think of anything else.

We were off.

Ro and I swept round each other, joined hands, and galloped sideways, just as everyone else did.

Then we swung in a circle with hands still joined.

Whoops and shouts.

We parted, stamped and, hands on hips, raised our heads like proud horses.

Now all the women joined hands, and we did light tapping steps on the spot, while the men looked on haughtily.

Then we stood back and clapped to the rhythm of the dance, and the men pretend-fought, in pairs.

On Ro's right was Badger, who now accidentally hit Ro on the nose. (This is *not* meant to happen.)

Ro dropped back, spluttering, and crashed into

the man on his left – Mehmed – and Mehmed's pretend foe.

'Hey – you tronker—'

Stumbling, Mehmed trod on another man's foot. This man wasn't bandit or Peshamban. His head was shaved except where hair, tied in a horse's tail, flared from the back. And he gave a roar and smacked his fist, painted blue, into Mehmed's face.

Next second three or four men were rolling on the ground, swearing and kicking, with two bandit women, and a girl, also shaven and horse-tailed, trying to separate and/or hit-them-with-a-nasty-looking metal-studded sash.

The Hulta girls, used to brawls, started laughing. But some of the Peshambans down the line looked upset. The dance had come all undone, though the band was still playing.

Next moment a space opened in the crowd, just the way the wind had blown on the plain through all the flowers.

I'd seen more of the watching crystals that turned, up on buildings. They did watch, for now through the parting of people and orange trees, came marching six of the clock-work doll-guards from the gates.

'Oops,' said Teil.

Toy said, gloomily, 'Now we're for it.'

To my horror I noted two of the doll-guards had *rifles* pointed right at us all.

Then another voice shouted loudly as a trumpet. I didn't recognize it, I'd never heard it before. It sounded made of brass.

But instantly somehow Ro and Mehmed scrambled up out of the muddle, leaving the horsetail man and another one flailing on the ground.

The doll-guards had reached us.

From out of a clockwork chest, a harsh unhuman voice ordered:

'*Cease fighting.*'

'I have,' said Ro, annoyed.

'Shut *up*,' muttered Mehmed, who had a blue smear on his cheek from the horsetail man's fist.

However, the horsetail man, and the other one, rolled apart, and sprang to their feet. They stared in alarm at the guards.

A silence settled, as the band gave up.

The deadly doll now demanded something – the same something, I think, over and over, in what seemed many different laguages. Which sounded very frightening. Finally '*Are you at peace now?*' demanded the deadly doll.

'Sure, yes, completely. Love everybody, eh Mehm?'

'Love 'em, yeah.'

The horsetail man, and the other one, had already mumbled something at other points in the language performance. Doubtless also saying how they loved everyone.

Then a man in scarlet and gold moved in between

us and the rifles. He was breathing fast from running down the line of dancers. And from shouting.

'A misunderstanding,' he said to the dolls with rifles and axes. 'I sincerely apologize. It won't happen again.'

I hadn't recognized his voice in the battle-bellow which stopped Ro and Mehmed as nothing else could. Now too it was different – like poured cream.

And the rifles were being lowered.

'*Do no harm in Peshamba,*' said the doll. '*Peshamba does no harm to you.*'

The weirdest thing. Some of the oranges on the orange trees flew open, and little coloured clockwork birds flew out of them, and up into the lamplight, to circle round and round. Just a coincidence, possibly.

I was taken aback anyway. But the guards had turned around and were marching neatly away again.

The horsetail girl fetched the horsetail man a ringing smack across his face. He cowered. What she was hissing at him I couldn't understand, thank goodness.

Ro and Mehmed laughed.

The music started once more, and the crowd was closing over like a repaired split seam. And the dance began again, again taking me by surprise.

It was apparently time to change partners as well.

The magnificent man in red grasped my hands, and whirled me away down the avenue of dancers, before I had time to wonder if now I'd *really* forgotten the steps.

CHANGING PARTNERS

'*I* didn't cause it.'

'I'd take a bet you did. You're trouble, girl.'

We paused to swing around hand in hand.

The lines of men and women clapped in time to the music.

He was smiling.

Argul.

I'd never seen him look so sensational. His hair was like black Peshamban silk. The colour red suited him. All that gold—

And now he took me by the waist and lifted me high in the dance — steps I truly didn't know — I couldn't do a thing, just stare down at his smiling, marvellous face. His teeth, in that tawny face, are so white—

He looks happy tonight. He looks *alive*.

I couldn't help laughing. I put my head back and laughed at the spinning starry sky.

When he set me on my feet, he steadied me, helped me get my balance again, but all the time we were still dancing . . .

The dance had changed in fact.

It was a Peshamban dance the girls had shown me. You move quite slowly, holding hands, taking easy, simple steps. Looking into each other's faces.

This was the dance I'd been afraid no one would want to choose me for.

'I don't mean to be trouble,' I said.

'Oh Claidi,' he said, 'you can't help it. Don't try. It's what a bird like you's good at.' I frowned. But I didn't care. Although he was insulting me, they didn't feel like insults. He said, 'Don't change. You're wonderful.'

The music of the dance had a song. It was something about the moon in a cloud. And getting lost in the cloud of the moon.

Sky so dark now, and the stars behind his head. The lamps, and the little mechanical birds flying.

Everyone enjoying themselves, yet far away. The mood of the night like rosy curtains in the background.

I thought, I *Know* this person. I know him as well as I know myself. But I didn't know him. I don't know myself.

We danced every dance.

Sometimes there were dances where we were separated. But we always met up again. Then he caught hold of me strongly. I felt I couldn't go wrong then.

I've never felt like that before.

Maybe I never will again.

At midnight, and midnight came so quickly, the CLOCK does something magical.

Not much warning. The band stopped playing. And everyone in the square, following the lead of the local Peshambans, raised their heads to look at the CLOCK.

Suddenly there was a strange noise, like a gigantic key turning in a lock. And then tinkly music began to drift down from the tall white tower.

The three figures on the CLOCK started to move.

The girl twirled, dancing as I had. The man bowed, and stretched out his hand to stroke the horse with the crystal horn, which, at that moment opened its wings.

And then they glided away behind the CLOCK, and other figures emerged from the other side. There was an old man leaning on a stick, and an Old Lady in a high head-dress, and a monstrous beast. It had the body of a lion and a tail like three snakes knotted together, and the head of a bird.

The old man regally raised his stick, in greeting, and the Old Lady raised her slender hands. And the beast opened its mouth and *fire* came out, cascades of yellow sparks.

In the crowd below lots of people cried out in surprise. But the Peshambans only sighed with joy, looking up with loving eyes at the CLOCK which was their god.

I whispered to Argul, 'It's amazing. But do they really worship it?'

'Yes,' he said.

'Why?'

'Because they say it's beautiful, and God is beautiful.'

Somehow this wasn't, at that moment, confusing.

'I see,' I said. I thought I did.

'And,' said Argul, 'they say this, the clock needs only a little attention to keep it working, and that's all religion needs too.'

'Religion . . .'

'Their worship of it, belief in it. Only a little work to keep perfection perfect.'

The music faded, and the three new figures became still. They're the figures that face the city from midnight to sunrise. Then they change again, but silently.

When the CLOCK had finished its display, and the Peshambans who were praying had stopped (prayer isn't only for rage or dismay. It seems to be just happiness, sometimes) Argul brought me a goblet of green wine.

Suddenly I could see why I'd thought him, that first time, so terrible, terrifying – he's so strong, so powerful. So *there*.

After that we walked up through the city, beyond the square and the CLOCK. I don't think we discussed why.

161

The streets were hung with trees, and cool, and smelled of flowers and scented dust and darkness.

There was another park. Peach-tinted lamps drooped from boughs.

We sat on a marble bench shaped like a bush under a large bush that had been cut and combed into the shape of a chair.

'Oh, *look*,' I said, 'another mechanical doll!'

It was a fantastic bird, gleaming blue in the park lamplight. It had all at once lifted its drifting tail and opened it like a fan of green and turquoise, purple and gold—

'No, Claidi. It's a peacock.'

'It's real?'

'Yes. As real as you.'

'I don't feel real tonight. I never knew cities existed any more.'

'When I was a child,' he said, 'my mother told me about Peshamba.'

'Did she?'

'There's something written on the face of the clock. You can only see it from the top of the tower. It says: *There's time enough for everything*.'

'Is there?'

'I hope so,' he said.

Testingly, I said, 'I haven't met your mother, have I?'

'No. She died eight years ago, when I was ten.'

I felt tremendously sorry. It was true. And now it reminded me of Twilight, my own lost mother.

'That's so sad.'

'Sad for the ones she left behind. She knew such a lot. Herbs, and chemicals. Some of them, now, call her the Witch. But she wasn't that. She understood science. Though she did have second sight.'

'What's that?'

'She could see things the others couldn't. Sometimes the future. She gave me—' he made a gesture towards his collar. Then stopped. 'A charm, or so we call it now. But it's scientific. It can tell you things.'

'I remember it,' I said. 'It's made of glass.'

'No. It just seems to be.'

'You were looking at it . . .' I hesitated, 'that time – when I thought – you were going to rob us.'

'We're not bandits, Claidi,' he said. 'We get called that. I won't say we've never thieved, but only to protect our own people, and never from people who hadn't got enough themselves. And we've fought and killed for the same reason. But not from choice. Do you believe me?'

'Yes.'

He looked at me for some time. The moon had risen late, it was in the sky. His dark eyes seemed more intense. Or the moon . . . was in a cloud, perhaps.

'I saw you first,' he said, 'in that dry old park in Chariot Town. You were with him, your posh lordly friend.'

163

'Nemian.'

'That one, yes.'

'I didn't see you—'

'No. It was just me and Blurn, out for a stroll. We trade with Sheepers, but we don't always trust them. We were just making sure of the town before any of the others came in later. We looked – a bit different.'

'And you *saw* me?'

'Yes.'

He didn't add anything, so I said, 'You didn't realize I was going to be bartered to the Feather Tribe.'

'You'd left by the time I did. Then we came after you.'

'Why?' I said.

'Why do you think?'

I said, humbly, 'Because you help people.'

I wanted him to say, of course, 'I did it because you're so incredible, Claidi.'

He wouldn't. He stared down his nose at me, his eyes burning and the moon pale in the trees behind his head.

What he did say was this, 'Why don't you stay with us? You're a pleasure to watch with Sirree, a natural rider. And you look your best in Hulta clothes. We live well. We look after our own, and others, when we can. You don't have to be afraid of anything with us. Not be hungry or thirsty. Or in danger. We travel. We go everywhere there is. Did you know there are enormous seas, Claidi? You do? Miles of just water and sky. And animals so odd you'd scream. Join our Family, Claidi. Stay.'

Thud, thud, my heart in my throat.

Couldn't speak.

I thought of Nemian, and the House. Of the ones I'd trusted and shouldn't have trusted.

'I—' I said.

The moon turned blue and winked away like a closing eye. Distracted, I stared at it, and then a wash of icy cold sank over me, over the world.

Something like wet silver spat into my face.

Argul stood up. He pulled me up too.

'What is it?'

'*Snow*. Damned *weather*.'

'What's—'

'Tell you later. Now we run.'

The park was full of flying figures, shrieking and yelps. Wild laughter, too. So many couples thinking only of each other, and then this—

White hurtled from the sky.

Soon we were running through a blanket. It was like feathers. That awful sacrificial dress, plucked and flung in my face.

On the square, when we reached it – rushing figures everywhere – people were carrying the orange trees indoors out of the cold.

I wanted to carry the night indoors in the same way.

165

But the night was flying off from us. This was a new dance. It was too fast.

We ran together as far as the Traveller's Rest. Hand in hand. I think there were streets.

But the Rest was like a full-stop, with lights in it. Windows blazed. Shouts and thunders. Everything was in turmoil.

'Claidi – I'll meet you here tomorrow. One hour after sun-up. By that tree. Yes?'

'Yes – yes—'

Into the dance of the snow, Argul vanished.

In the morning, that tree, which he'd said we would meet by, and which had been shaped like a candle flame of green, was *white*, a round white ball, from the snow.

That's how things can change. Overnight.

Anyway, they changed before I saw the tree in the morning.

After I got upstairs that night, to the womens' bedroom, I found it was empty.

I wished Argul hadn't had to go, but he would be seeing to things, making sure of the horses. Blurn would have gone too. I expected Blurn's girlfriend felt as I did. Did that mean Argul and I—?

Really I couldn't work it out.

So I stood at the window, watching the snow falling on Peshamba, settling in white heaps everywhere, changing things. And quietness came. I never heard such quiet.

166

Snow had never fallen in the Garden. Perhaps it doesn't happen in that area, or the Garden was kept too warm.

To be honest I felt happy. And scared. I wondered if I'd imagined things had happened that hadn't. The way he looked at me. He hadn't said anything about my being with him. He'd simply suggested I stay with the Hulta.

And I wanted to. Did I? Yes. But – you see, I'd rushed off with Nemian from the only life I knew. And I'd loved Nemian. And now I was ready to rush off again in another direction, and was that any more sensible than the first time? And was all my life going to be like this, rushing from one place, one person, to another? Exciting – maybe. Also exhausting, and fruitless.

The snow fell and my thoughts swam round and round, and then someone knocked on the door.

When they didn't come in, I went and opened it.

I jumped back in – well, sort of horror really. It was Nemian.

He'd bought or found new clothes. Black and gold. He looked striking and painfully handsome. He was very pale.

'Claidi – can I come in? Or will you come out for a minute?'

'There's no one else here,' I unwisely said.

I let him walk into the room.

He glanced round. Bandit – no, Hulta – womens' stuff everywhere.

Nemian looked back at me.

'Did you have a nice evening?' I asked acidly.

'Not really. I was looking for you.'

'I wasn't so far off.'

'Perhaps not.' He paused. He said, 'I wasn't playing about today, Claidi. I was trying to find ballooneers. Peshamba used to have balloons for travel. Not any more.'

I nodded. I tried to look polite and vague, but a flaming fierceness, chilly and desperate, seemed all over Nemian, sizzling in the air.

'Claidi – I know what you think of me.'

'Do you?'

'You think I'm a skunk.'

'What's a skunk?'

'Claidi, don't start that.' (I felt and must have looked annoyed. I didn't know what a skunk *was*.) 'Claidi, that girl—'

'Mm? Which girl?'

'You know which girl. I'm sorry. It just – happened.'

'Well, lovely,' I said. I smiled my best congratulatory smile.

Then he really astonished me.

He dropped on one knee in front of me, and seized both my hands.

'Claidi, don't play with me. I know I deserve it. But – all this has been so strange for me. I've been confused. I didn't think it through – and now – Claidi, tell me I haven't lost you.'

He really is beautiful. The snowlight burned on his hair. I trembled, without quite knowing why.

'Lost me?' I asked casually. 'How do you mean?'

'You *will* go on with me, to my city on Wide River? I have to know you will – Oh Claidi – Claidi, I'll lose everything if I lose you. Please forgive my hopeless mindless stupidity. Stay with me. Come with me.'

I swallowed. I couldn't think what to say. Can you just say *No* in a case like this?

He was sweating. His eyes – had *tears* in them.

He wrung my hands like washing and only loosened his grip when I squeaked '*Ow!*'

'There *is* a method of transport,' he said, 'not a balloon. Precarious, rather. But I'll look after you. I promise I will, Claidi.'

'Er. But—' I faltered. Well, you know, I never claimed to be intelligent.

'Claidi, in my city, my grandmother is very, very old. Like Jizania. And I have to get back to her. And to my duties there. I'm a prince. My life isn't entirely my own. You'll know.' (He'd forgotten again, I thought, about whether I truly am royal.) 'And this life of mine, Claidi, frankly isn't worth anything, if I can't take you with me. I *need* you. If only I can make you understand.'

And then he stood up and dropped my hands with absolute snow-cold dignity.

'It's your choice, of course. And I don't deserve

169

anything from you. I've been an absolute fool. Shall I go now?'

In the silence then, in the corridor outside, we heard the soft laughter and footfalls of the Hulta women coming back to the room.

At the agreed time, I stood in the snow by the white ball that had been a tree.

Kids were out, throwing snow at each other. The horsetail men and women were charging their zebras up and down. Chimneys I'd never noticed puffed up blue, and there was a smell of hot bread, and bells rang sweetly.

Argul came towards me over the white. It was miraculous, just watching him. I let myself pretend. Just for a minute.

And as he reached me, and saw my face, and his altered, darkened, closed in, I said, 'I'm sorry, Argul, but I can't stay.' He stood there then. Silent. 'I thought I could, and I wanted to, but now – the situation seems very serious. I have to go on.'

'With him,' said Argul. A storm went through the back of his eyes. He shook his head. The storm was gone.

'As you know,' I said primly, 'we've travelled together this far, Nemian and I.'

Argul said, 'He's an okk.'

I blinked.

'You don't like him.'

'Oh, I love him.' Argul's eyes on mine. I had to

look down. He said, 'No, excuse me. You're the one does that.'

Then he turned and walked away, striding off across the snow, and as he did, something dropped from his hand.

It wasn't until one of the kids ran over and picked it up, and it sparkled, that I saw it was a ring with a brilliant stone. Had it been for me? Surely . . . not.

The children ran away with it, after him. They were Peshamban, and very honest, and I think it was a diamond.

MARSHES OF THE MOON

Some time has gone by, before I came back to this book to write any more. We're at a place called River Jaws, and have to wait a day or something, for something or other. I forget why or what.

The ink pencil ran out, too (I've written enough to use up a whole one.) And I'd forgotten to ask Teil for more, so had nothing to write with.

He gave me a sort of pen-thing, his, I suppose, only it doesn't write quite the same. Which some-how makes writing not so easy.

Or am I only making excuses?

Yes, Claidi, I hear you say, you are.

When he said, I mean Nemian, 'So you're still writing in your book,' I was afraid he'd want to read it. But he doesn't seem interested. I think he just thinks I like doing it. He called it my *Diary*. He said lots of 'ladies' keep diaries in his city. So it's fashionable, so it's all right. Perhaps helps convince him I'm royal.

He's been attentive. But also he looks – nervous? If he wants me, then maybe that's all it is. But he doesn't touch me, now.

I feel sorry for Nemian. I try to be friendly and cheerful, to show him I'm all right, and I like him, and I do *try* to like him.

I don't *dis*like him.

But I can't feel the way I did. I wish I could.

Why else did I leave Argul and the Hulta? It's hard to explain. I wanted to stay with the ban— the Family. But it was about what I'd felt before. That I'd kept changing my mind.

You can see, I hope, how I felt. Disloyal. I *don't* want to rush from person to person, never knowing who I'm going to want next. Like some spoilt horrible little child.

The people in the House were always doing that. Now they were friends with X, then with Y, then with Z. And then they had an argument with Z and went back to X. Revolting.

I'm not like that. I hope I'm not. Nemian was the one I chose to be with. All right, he behaved badly, but then, I'm just Claidi. He got distracted from me. Not too difficult, I expect.

I have to be loyal to him. I chose him first. If I can't trust my own feelings, my own self—

That was what I wanted, to be loyal. To prove to myself I'm not a shallow, silly, worthless little idiot.

So I did what I did.

The Hulta acted oddly to me. Not nasty, just fed up and a bit short. Only Teil said good-bye. Dagger came up and *confronted* me. She looked terribly fierce. 'Why are you going with *him*?' she demanded.

Tried to explain. The loyalty thing. Nemian. She snorted like a horse. She said, 'You're mad.' And some other words I shouldn't have been surprised she knew.

It doesn't make sense, yet it does. Doesn't it. Of course it does. Yes. I'll be glad later, when we get to the city.

He was so definite, how much he needs me.

Argul doesn't. (That ring, it wasn't for me.) He's got all the Hulta, loving him and loyal to him. He even knew his mother.

Nemian and I – I'll do the best I can. Please God, even if you're a CLOCK, help me to do the best I can.

The first part of the journey from Peshamba was fairly ordinary, except for the snow.

All the plains about the city were white, like book paper with nothing written there. I wondered if the flowers would survive. Probably somehow they do, for obviously snows have happened before.

(In fact, the lake had gone solid, frozen, and they were sliding on it and 'skating'.)

Nemian gave me a big fur cloak. He said it didn't come from an animal, but that the Peshambans can make these garments, like pelts. It was warm.

We rode in a chariot again, one of three, but drawn by donkeys. They had red blankets and little bells.

Jingle jingle.

When I looked back, a blue haze floated over the city on the pale grey luminous sky, from all the smokes.

There was hot tea and mulled wine in flasks. But it got cold quickly and wasn't so nice.

For several days we were in the plains.

Once we saw some large white things, like clouds, blowing slowly along. Nemian told me they were elephants. They grow thick woolly coats like sheep, in the cold, and have noses like tails. That sounds crazy, and maybe he made it up to amuse me. We weren't near enough to see for sure.

At night there were tents put up. I had one to myself. Iron baskets had burning coals in for heat.

I sat and re-read this book, or bits of it.

I don't seem quite the same person now as when I started it. That makes sense? Who the hell am I?

Finally, although it can't have been that long, the

weather started to alter, and so did the landscape. I could see enormous hills, mountains, appearing far to the left. It felt warmer almost at once.

The sky began to break open in cracks of blue. Then it was all blue with cracks of white.

There were grasses again, but very tall, higher in parts than the chariots. (The donkeys tended to eat their way through, chewing as they trotted.) There was a trackway, and then we reached a large village or small town.

Normally I'd have been interested, but I wasn't very. I'm useless. On this extraordinary adventure, and wasting it all.

Let's see. There were round-sided houses, and fields where they kept having to hack the grass back from the grain. Weird trees with boughs that hung right down to the ground, like tents, and huge black and pink birds rumbling about in them making quacking noises.

They had a stream, which rushed, and was white with foam.

Everyone else stopped in the village-town, and only Nemian and I got a boat with a boat-driver (apparently you don't call them that, but what?) and we set off down the stream. Although we'd stayed a couple of nights in the town-village, Nemian didn't go rushing off with everyone, although, again, he could speak their language. (They also take money for things, and he paid them.)

He'd started to tell me where we were going.

Through marshes, he said. The people there are odd, but would provide the means to take us to the River.

I had this awful feeling, which had begun on the plains, and now was getting stronger and stronger. It was a sort of fear, and a sort of ache. Later on, Nemian, who had also begun talking to me regularly, said he'd felt 'homesick' for his city. And I realized then that I'm homesick. But not for any place.

I used to see him every day. Argul. You could always expect to see him. Riding along the wagons, checking stores, at the fire by night. (I didn't often speak to him. Didn't think he noticed me.) Or I'd seen him wrestling with his men, or playing cards – he could do very clever card tricks – magic tricks, too. Once, on the flower plains, he produced a sparrow out of Teil's ear. Couldn't work out how he did it – a real sparrow, which flew away. Or when they took turns singing, he'd sing. Not that well, actually. You always could see him, doing something. Or just there.

Just there.

(I've been trying to work out how long the journey has taken so far, from the House, to this house, overlooking the River. I've got muddled though. It seems to have gone on for ever.)

It was sunset when we reached the marshes, and

the stream, which had got wider and slower, with islands of the tall grass, became eventually choked with reeds.

The boat-driver (I never did learn his proper title) poled us carefully between. The low sun glinted red and copper on the water, all striped with reed shadows.

Out of this somehow-mournful picture, a building rose, not very cheery either. Black stone, with pillars and a strange up-pointing roof.

Nemian told me it was a shrine. Ah. I knew about shrines. (?) This one was in honour of the marsh god.

But when we landed at the water-steps, and climbed cautiously – they were slippery and very old – up them, there was an image of the god on a black slab. I thought at first it was another clock, but it wasn't. They worship the moon, to which, they say, there, the marshes belong.

'Why?' I said. I've never stopped asking questions. If that stops, frankly I think I'm done for.

'The Wide River lies over beyond the marshes. It's tidal, and so are they.'

'Tidal. Like seas?'

Apparently so. They drain and fill, affected by the pull of the moon. So, the moon's a god, in the marshes.

Later, when we were in the hall of the shrine, a gloomy old place and no mistake, eating some gloomy bread and bitter crumbly (gloomy) cheese,

I spoke to Nemian about this thing of God and gods.

'God is everything,' he said. 'Gods, individual gods, I mean, are expressions of God. As we are.'

'We're *part* of God?' I goggled. I'd begun to have great respect for this (unknown) and super-astonishing Being.

'God gave us life,' said Nemian, simply.

He looked so special, and so quiet and sad, and what he said, the way he'd explained or tried to, (God may be inexplicable, I somehow guess) I could see Argul in Nemian. Just for a second. So different, like the voice, the accent. But.

I put my hand on his. I hadn't been very nice to him. Not affectionate or flattered, after he'd gone down on his knees. (Well, one knee anyway.)

He glanced at me. And he smiled. He seemed suddenly very pleased, delighted, excited.

And I was flattered after all.

Perhaps it might be all right?

'Claidi, can I ask you a favour?'

Cautious as on the stairs, I nodded.

'I'd like to get back to calling you by your full name.'

'Oh.'

'When we reach my City, they'll expect it. In public. You'll be treated as you should be, as someone important, vital. And *Claidi* is a bit – not quite dignified enough, is it.'

'Really.'

'Don't be angry, Claidi – Claidissa, may I?'

'All right. But, I'll have to get used to it.'

It isn't me. So, more confusion. Who's this Claidissa woman?

We were at the shrine of the moon until moon-rise, when one of the shadowy people there told us the Riders had come.

Out we went, and there below the water-steps I saw this:

Over the dark marshes, the dark sky and the moon. And in the water between the reeds, enormous lizards, coloured the dark red of a Garden-bred rose. Some just lay there, wallowing, as the hippos had done in the Garden river. But others had openwork cages strapped on their backs, and men were sitting in these.

What I'd expected I can't say. I wouldn't have got it right, whatever it was.

'What are—?'

'They're alligators, Claidissa. And those things on their backs are riding-jadaja.'

'Ja-daja. I see.'

The alligators, some of them, flickered their tails. All their red scales skittered moonlight. They were very beautiful, but their eyes were cold and shone a moonish green.

The moon did have a green tinge too. A sort of vapour was wisping up the sky, wrapping over it. The moon in a cloud – lost in the cloud of the moon. Or just lost in the marshes of the moon.

179

'What fun,' I depressedly said.

But then the Riders were slipping off, all agile, on to the steps. They carried things to offer the moon-god. Things they'd shot with arrows mostly, in the marsh.

People have to eat. I suppose they have to make offerings, too. But it looked pretty dismal.

Nemian, to my amazement, couldn't speak the language of the Alligator Riders. Someone from the shrine had to help. At last, something was agreed, and then an alligator was guided by its Rider up to the steps, and somehow we stepped on it, and got into the quite-big cage, and sat down on its padded floor.

I wondered if these people used money. Decided they might not. Their hair was unevenly cut short and they wore reed-woven garments. (Nemian told me after, at the time I could only see they looked rough and ready.) Their jewellery consisted of polished pebbles, alligator claws and teeth.

The cage jadaja thing was also made from reeds.

Our Rider didn't seem to mind not calling in at the shrine. Perhaps they consider it part of their worship of the moon, to assist travellers who meet them by moonlight.

As he guided his beast away, by gentle kicks and pats on its sides, the Rider began to sing, raising his eyes to the moon.

The moon was green in its veil. Mists rose from the marshes. The water glimmered like old glass.

His miserable-sounding song, with its no-doubt-miserable unknown words, made me want to howl like one of the Hulta's dogs, only they seldom had.

We were in the marshes a few days and nights. We stopped off at tiny villages of reed houses, where people sat fishing or mending nets, and the women wove cloth from reeds, at reed-built looms.

A silent people. They didn't say much to each other. Nemian communicated by signals. They gave us fish and edible leaves and unpleasant-tasting water that must have been all right.

The mouth of an alligator is one man-length long. Or a little longer. They have about three million teeth, or so it looked. But I saw Rider children swimming around with them, diving under the water with them. Even toddlers.

Alligators smell fishy. Or these did.

We did, soon.

One sunset, I must describe it. Some salts in the marsh sometimes cause weird colours. But the sky went lavender, and the sun was ginger. And these tones mixed in the water. Lightning fluttered, dry, without rain or wind or thunder. And the lightning was rainbow-coloured, and in shapes – like branching trees, like bridges, like rolling wheels.

He said, 'It's pretty. I've never seen this, although I've heard of it. Marsh lightning. It's nothing, of course, to City fireworks.'

181

When we got here, to River Jaws, was yesterday. The marsh ends here, and from the upper storey of the guest-house, if it is, you can see over the lines and ranks of reeds, to an endless sheet of water. Wide River.

It does sink down and rise up, tidal, as he said.

They seem to be servants here. They speak the language I do, and some other language. Nemian can speak both of these.

The reason we're waiting: Nemian sent someone from here to arrange another boat.

No sooner did I write that, than Nemian came by, just now, and enthusiastically told me we'll leave tomorrow.

In three days, he enthused, we'll be there. In his City with the fireworks and the Wolf Tower. His home. Mine.

HIS CITY

Wide River's wide. One seems to drift, in the middle of space, or the sky. Because the sky reflects in the River, and they become one. And there's only the boat, no land on either side.

A huge curved sail, filling slowly with steady, *breathing* wind. Like a lung.

They were slaves. I mean, the people who waited on us. I'd never been waited on, the opposite, of course. I wasn't keen on it. And, they were slaves,

182

not servants. Two men and a woman, who sat in the boat's back – its *stern* – cross-legged, heads down, ready for Nemian to call or snap his fingers.

Also there were two sailors, to drive the boat. (Or, it was a ship, I think.) Very respectful. No, they grovelled.

Feeling so uncomfortable with this, I spent a lot of time sitting by the side, staring out.

Sunset the first night was glorious.

'Look at all the gold,' I said to Nemian. Every so often I tried to speak to him.

'If you like that, I think I can really please you,' said Nemian.

Baffled, I let him take me to the cabin room where I was to sleep. The slave woman was there, and bowed almost to her knees.

'The Princess Claidissa,' said Nemian, 'will be shown the dress now.'

So then the poor old slave undid a chest and brought out this dress.

Even in the House, I admit, I never saw a dress quite so magnificent. In the wild light reflecting off sky and River, the golden tissue of the dress seemed made of fire.

'That's what you'll wear,' announced Nemian, 'when we sail into my City.'

I was meant to be thrilled, and thank him, and tweet with delight.

Well, I did thank him.

'It's a very grand dress.'

'Oh I know you prefer simple clothes,' said Nemian, kindly, 'Jizania told me about that. I even do believe you used to polish the odd table or whatever it was. You're a funny little thing. But in public, you'll need to dress up.'

Obviously, not to let him down. That was fair. He was bringing me back, showing me off. I had to be acceptable to them. It was worrying, all this. If I was to be with him – I mean *be* with him as a companion, perhaps a wife (I'd never been sure) I'd have to be responsible. Take pains.

Princess Claidissa.

Oh.

'Oh,' I said, quite humbly.

We had dinner on the deck, waited on hand and foot, arm and leg, as it were. Wine and fruit and dishes under silver covers.

Rather like the House.

What had I expected?

Maybe, at the start, I'd even wanted it, to be served, have things done for *me*. What other system had I ever been shown – it was either lord it, or live as a slave.

Since then . . .

I chatted brightly. Oh, see, there were birds flying over. Oh, look, there was an island with a tree.

Dusk went to night. I went in to sleep. Couldn't.

It was almost four days, in the end. The wind was often slow, the tides made it take longer, or something. They said these things to him, apologizing, acting bothered in case he got angry. But Nemian, thank God, was just off-hand and idle with them, only slightly impatient once or twice. Never rude or vicious or violent.

On the last day, the land began to appear regularly on either side. But the weather had changed. It got chilly. The skies, the water, were two silk sheets of grey.

Then clouds came, and rain fell in tired little sprinkles.

Just after lunch, a tall, tall, smooth, slim, grey stone appeared, standing on the nearer bank – we could now see both of them. There wasn't much else. A few trees, trailing down into the water, and a flattish plain, with thin mountain shapes on the left that must be months in the distance. (Altogether rather a bare sort of place, it seemed.)

'Ah!' cried Nemian though, and jumped up.

He saluted the pillar, or whatever it was, standing very straight, just as *it* was. And all the slaves and boat-slaves bowed over double.

Nemian turned to me. His face was alight with energy.

'Only an hour or so more, Claidissa. Then we'll be there.'

I felt immediately sick. This seemed ridiculous. I should be interested, at least.

'I'm so glad,' I said.

'Go and get ready now, Claidissa.'

'Oh, but—'

'It's all right. I'll change on deck in that tent thing. Just concentrate on yourself.'

In fact I'd been going to say I wouldn't need 'an hour or so' to get ready. But it wouldn't matter, really, so I did what he said, and the woman slave followed me into the cabin.

How wrong I was. It did take all of two hours.

First washing, and hair-washing, and drying, and then perfumes and things. All fine, only I felt peculiar, so it wasn't.

Then the slave dressed me in lace undies, and slid me into the golden dress.

After that stockings and shoes, bracelets, earrings. (Even a gold bag for this book.) My hair was still damp, but the slave began to arrange it. Parts were plaited, and bits were put up with pins, and some hung down in curls that were made with two heated iron sticks – tongs, she said – and there was a nasty smell of scorched hair – mine.

She made up my face. She put on powder, and dark round the eyes, and blush for the mouth and cheeks.

She even coloured my fingernails with gold, and I had to sit there like an insane sort of tree, holding out my hands, fingers stretched apart to let the stuff dry.

When I got back on the deck, Nemian was standing there in his black and gold, looking regal. He gave me a nod. Which seemed mean after the two hour preparation. He could have said, I thought, How nice you look, or something. Even if only for the slave's benefit, she'd worked so hard.

The slaves served us yellow wine in tall glasses.

And the City appeared.

I'd been thinking, uneasily, how dreary it all looked, all this flattish greyishness, with higher greyish things – I didn't know what – starting to poke up. There was a vague rain-mist. Everything looked ghostly.

And then this enormous *heap* swelled up and closed in all around.

Out of the mist reared a gigantic black statue. It was slick with rain, gleaming. What was it? It seemed to be a frowning man, his head raised high into the mist.

I was still puzzling over it, but other shapes, all completely huge, were now pushing in behind, and the ship-boat floated as if helpless in among them.

High stone banks rose from the river. Up from these piled terraces of dark buildings, stone on stone. And towers loomed in the sky, softened only by the mist. From one or two windows, a faint light seeped. They glistened though, in the wet, like dark snakes.

And everywhere, the gigantic statues, in pale marble, or black basalt. Rearing beasts, (lions, bears (?)) A grim stone woman leaned down toward the River so I thought for a moment (terrified) this statue was tumbling and would fall right on the boat. In her upstretched stone hand, a real (vast) mirror, which reflected our upturned faces, small as the faces of mice.

Roofs layered on the sky, vanished in mist and cloud. Everything was so big. So smooth and burnished. So clean and cold and dim and dark.

'Yes,' he breathed. 'I've missed this place. Home. My home. Yours. And look there – over there – can you see?'

I gazed where he pointed. And saw a tower that somehow managed to be even bigger than all the rest, and even smoother and dimmer and etc: On the top, a furious black stone thing crouched, snarling, one taloned paw upraised, and a flag in it, dark and limp in the rain.

So I didn't need him to say to me, in his emotional and exalting voice: '*The Wolf Tower.*'

Perhaps not unreasonably, since Nemian was important, and after all he'd said about a welcome, I'd expected crowds.

There weren't any. Or, only one.

The ship was guided in to the bank, and there, in a long stone porch that stretched from the Wolf Tower, with its demon wolf, were some people richly dressed, and a group of others, obviously more slaves.

These other slaves lay down on the pavement, in the puddles.

'Our' slaves on the ship lay down on the deck, even the one tying us up to the bank, once he'd finished.

The royalty approached the steps, and looked down at us. They wore fantastic clothes, thick with gold and silver, more like *armour*.

But they were smiling, and waving soft hands.

'Nemian – Nemian—' they cried, 'darling—'

They all looked alike to me, in a funny way. A lot of them had golden hair just like his.

Nemian got ashore and walked up the steps. Then he turned and gestured back towards me, showing me to them. And they clapped and gave little shrill cries.

I didn't know what I was supposed to do, so just stood there like a twerp.

One of the men said, 'Your messenger was here before you, Nemian, in good time. The Old Lady will come out.' Nemian coloured with pleasure. (His grandmother, must be.)

'I don't deserve it. I nearly failed you.'

'No, no, Nemian. We heard how things went wrong. And still you took success.'

They beamed at me. Should I smile too? Or stay ever so dignified? Before I could decide, a horn wailed from somewhere in the tower. *They* all fell deadly smileless and silent. Their heads all turned towards the door that opened on the porch. It was a high oblong door, of two steely halves.

Two slaves emerged first, holding out their arms, as if to shoo everyone aside. They looked haughty. Then she came out.

Instantly I knew her. Instantly again I didn't. I wished I hadn't drunk the wine.

She was tall, thin, *smoothed* like the buildings. She had their colours or non-colours.

No mistaking her eyes. Black in her dry elderly white face. They were glaring straight at me, as if to strip me to the bones.

The two haughty slaves yapped in chorus: 'Princess Ironel Novendot.'

And suddenly I knew who she reminded me of, for all her utter unlikeness: Jizania Tiger of the House I'd left behind.

THE LAW: FINDING

Looking around, for the thousandth time, I wonder if there's any way I can use that window, or that one, or even the door. Or is there anything I can do? I think about the million and one times at the House I got into hot water, and usually got myself out of it again. Maybe with a slapped face or bleeding beaten hands, but nothing too final. However, this is difficult. No. It's impossible. Argul told me I was trouble, or made trouble, and he was absolutely right. I just wish he was here to say, *I told you so*. Although I don't, really, wish he was here. I wouldn't wish many people *here*.

Sorry, I'll start again. You won't know yet what I'm on about.

When did I first start to panic? Well that was long before *this*. Really almost as soon as I saw the Princess Ironel.

She came walking along the stone porch, with her black liquorice cane tapping on the ground. Her hands were white claws.

She wasn't beautiful like Jizania, and Ironel had all her hair, partly black still, or iron-coloured, and pulled back off her mask-like face into a towering top-knot stuck with silver pins.

As she approached, Nemian and all the others kneeled down. Not one knee either, both knees.

And the slaves were flat, all but her slaves, who presently kneeled and bowed their heads.

But I stood upright, there on the boat-ship. Why? In a way, I was frightened of tearing the dress if I kneeled. (It seemed very flimsy material.) Or getting it dirty. I mean, it couldn't be mine. *They'd* provided it, this lot. (Just as maids had been dressed by the House.)

I did bow my head. But that was shame more than anything else.

And why was I ashamed? Second sight, maybe, like Argul's mum.

Sort of cricking my neck, I saw Ironel Novendot raise Nemian and embrace him. It was a stiff and a cold embrace. It was as if one of the towers did it. But he seemed awfully happy. He kissed her claws.

'You found her,' she said.

'Madam, I did.'

191

'What is her name?' I heard the old voice rasp. (Me?)

'Claidissa Star.' (Me.)

'Yes,' said Ironel Novendot. 'That is correct.'

The hairs rose on my scalp under all the curls and coilings. *What did she mean*? He'd *found* me? She *knew* me?

Then the appalling slaves on the boat were help-thrusting me up the stairs on to the bank and into the porch, and I was right in front of her.

'You are welcome to the City,' said the old woman. She spoke – as he had – as if only this City existed, capital C. Like the capital H of the House. All lies, as now I knew. 'We are very glad you've come,' she added. 'I, certainly.'

She. She didn't look it. Her *eyes*, jet black with grey rings round the black. Awful eyes. But she *did* look like Jizania, in a way. Was it just her age? No – and anyway, how old was she?

'We will go in now,' she told us.

An order.

Everyone got up, simpering.

She turned back to me, sudden as something springing, and caught my face in a bunch of claws.

'Do you speak?'

'Yes, madam.'

'Good.' She smiled. Ah. Her teeth were false. They were wonderful. Pearls set in silver. She must save that smile for very special moments. (She does.)

192

First of all, the slaves let us into a hollow in the wall, and closed a gilded gate. Then they worked a handle inside and the whole thing, hollow, gate, us, went rocking upwards. Walls shut us in on all sides. I didn't like it. But I recalled Nemian telling me about clockwork 'lifters' which could carry people to the top storeys of his City.

Just as I thought I'd go mad and scream, we reached another open hollow. To my horror, we went right up past it.

There were some more of these. When I'd given up hope, we came to a hollow and stopped. More slaves outside opened the gate.

Outside was a colossal hall. It seemed to go on for ever on every side, and the ceiling too was high as a sky, or looked like it. It was painted like a sky too, only the paint had faded. Unless they did it that way in the first place, grey, with grape-dark clouds. (Probably they did.)

On the deep grey marble expanse of floor were spindly tables with things to eat and drink, tobacco, and open boxes of strange stalks and tablets. These were like the things Nemian had given me instead of food in the dust desert. I couldn't see why they would be necessary here.

Nemian though took a handful of them, and ate them. Then he took some wine from a slave. So did I, the wine, although I didn't want it.

The old woman took only a glass of something that looked like muddy pond water, sucked it, and pulled a face like a kid who'd been given burnt spinach when it wanted an ice-cream.

But she clasped Nemian's arm. As they walked along the long, long floor away from the crowd – who all watched admiringly and went on simpering – she called, 'You, too, Claidissa.'

So I, too, went with them.

There were vast windows stretching floor to ceiling. They had glass in them, and eventually we stood at one, looking out over the City. (There was also something nasty bulging over the window top, twice my height again, over my head. Took me a while to realize it was one black *paw* of the evil wolf statue on the roof, curled down over the window. What a place!)

The City looked vile too. How could he be proud of it? Homesick for it?

Rain boiled among the stupid, too-high buildings. The depressing statues lurched and craned. Everything black or grey or like sour milk. Absolute rubbish.

I'd been vaguely wondering if there were any outer walls to guard it. (I've since learned there aren't. Instead they have look-outs and other things, like Peshamba, but more 'serious'.) But right then I thought just one look at this place would make anyone, friend or foe, turn round and trudge off in another direction. Any direction.

Nemian and his Gran had been murmuring things to each other. Not exactly loving, but sort of secretive and sneaky, somehow. They both had a sly, smug look. It didn't suit either of them. He didn't look so handsome. His face seemed to have changed. And glancing at me abruptly he laughed. It was a cruel laugh. One couldn't miss it. It was a laugh of heartless triumph.

I didn't want to make a judgement. I'd done a lot of that and been proved wrong. I just stood there meekly.

Ironel Novendot said to me, also glancing side-long, 'And how is Jizania these days?'

That was so much what had been on my mind, and I said at once, 'Blooming.'

'Blast the creature,' said Ironel, snapping her pearls spitefully. 'Wouldn't she just!'

'I'm afraid,' I said, sadly, 'she forgot to send you her regards.' (Forgot a lot of things, I mentally added. Like the fact she and you seem to know each other.)

But Ironel only sucked her drink again.

'One day,' she said to me, 'you too will have to live on muck like this. Has he told you my age?'

She waited. Old People often like you to be astounded by their ages. I said, 'No, madam.'

'One hundred and seventy,' she informed me.

Well, I didn't believe her. She wasn't more than ninety-nine, I'd have said. But I widened my eyes and exclaimed, 'A great age, lady.'

'You too,' she said, 'will reach a great age, here in our City. And you too will end as I am, drinking slops.' And she smiled again, pleased at the idea.

A curse?

No, it seemed to be simply a fact.

I went colder, far colder, than if she *had* cursed me.

Nemian said, 'She doesn't know yet, Grandmother.'

'Doesn't she? Nice surprise for her then. How did you get her here?'

Nemian shot me a little-boyish, rueful look. He seemed to be saying, I just know you'll forgive me, Claidi. He actually said, 'Well, madam, I lied to her a lot.'

'And with your pretty face,' said Ironel, happier by the second, 'the poor little fish was hooked.'

My mouth *didn't* fall open. And I *didn't* throw up on their shoes. I remain proud of both these things. I was so afraid, I felt as if I was floating in the air inside a ball of ice. Struck dumb, I couldn't question them. So I stayed mercifully silent.

Nemian said, 'When Jizania's people shot the balloon down – *not* in my plan – I thought I'd had it, I confess. But luck was on my side. And Jizania stuck to her vow – once I'd shown her the flower. It's just possible she might have forgotten, if I hadn't. Her mind isn't as sharp as *yours*, Grandmother.'

They smirked at each other.

Then Ironel said, 'I must show Claidissa the garden of Immortal flowers.'

I couldn't work any of it out. Sometime one of these monsters was going to have to explain it all to me. Not only had I been made a fool of, I was a fool to start with.

Strangely, I had then a sudden image of Argul. He'd never have been caught out by such people. He'd have known what was going on. But in such a situation, he would have been terrific, I just knew. This is hard to describe, but all at once, I seemed to myself to *become* Argul. I wasn't Claidi any more, but him, tall and strong, confident and clever. And brave.

I looked at them with Argul's eyes, and I said, 'This wine's rather bad, isn't it? Perhaps you're just used to it. But really.' And I upended the glass-full and poured it on their horrible floor.

They both *gaped* at me. What a sight.

At that moment, a bell rang.

Everyone looked, even they did. Through a gauzy curtain came two new slaves, bowing. And then this girl.

She was – I don't know where to begin. I'll try. If you took one new-born primrose and mixed its colour in the purest cream, that was her skin, the exact shade, and as smooth. She had black-blue eyes, slanting upward at the outer corners. She had *blue* – must have been black – hair that hung straight as sheet metal to the backs of her knees.

She wore white, and the rain must have drenched her and then turned to opals.

'Ah, now,' said the old witch, Ironel. 'Here's Moon Silk.'

This girl, Moon Silk, came along the floor, gliding on perfect moon–pale feet.

And Nemian gave a sort of strangled cry. And down his cheeks ran more rain, only this was tears.

He left me, he left his fearful grannie, and he strode to the exquisite girl and raised her into his arms. He kissed her. It was – a *kiss*.

Despite everything, it startles me to have to report, I felt as if I'd been hit in the stomach.

And Ironel said, not needing to, as he hadn't needed to name this awful Tower, 'How touching. Lovers re-meeting. Nemian and his young bride. They were only married, Claidissa, a month, before he had to leave us on his quest for *you*.'

She told me. (Ironel.) She must have loved it. I tried to be Argul, still, but he'd never have got in this mess. In the end I just had to be Claidi, and listen, and cope as best I could.

It's soon told, though she went on and on, embroidering bits lovingly. Lingering. Watching me to see if I'd cry or jump about.

Before, she took me with her, alone, along the top storey of the Wolf Tower. From various windows she pointed out ugly important buildings.

The other three Towers, for example, in the three other quarters of the City. They are the Pig Tower, the Vulture Tower, and the Tiger Tower. You'll probably see at once, the Tiger Tower used to be Jizania Tiger's. Where Jizania was *born*.

Ironel also showed me a courtyard in which, in four grey stone vases, grew the brilliant red flowers with juicy leaves. One of which Nemian handed Jizania in the House Debating Hall.

Meanwhile, downstairs, in the Wolf Tower, Nemian would be blissfully alone with his wife. Moon Silk. Ironel kept going back to that.

But she slipped up there. In the end, I got used to it.

Let's face it, too, he was a rotten husband. Married one month, and the moment he had the chance, off with a Hulta girl. He'd led me on because he had to. But there was no excuse for *that*.

We were by then seated in Ironel's apartment in the Tower, in another far-too-large room, that echoed. Outside was a view of where the River grew hugely wide again, and the opposite bank wasn't to be seen.

The Wolf Tower isn't very warm. They don't have the heating system the House had. Just fireplaces and baskets of coals, (braziers) both of which smoke.

Anyway, I must now write down what Ironel Novendot told me. Because this book is the story of my life, and she – or the Law of the Tower – made it all happen.

Yes. The *Law*.

But I think I'll have to explain about that separately. It's a story in itself, the Wolf Tower Law. I've only become a tiny desperate bit of it.

The Law (and as I say, I'll go back to the Law) decreed that Nemian had to find a girl to take over a particular duty in the City. Probably the most necessary duty. And that was because Ironel, who until now had seen to this duty, was at last too old for it – or she said she was.

And here Law is LAW. Is Absolute. No one goes against it.

So Nemian, just married and all, set off in the hot-air balloon, of which the City has a fleet, although they seldom use them.

Some things then went wrong with the balloon, and there was a chance he wouldn't make it. Then he did make it, only to be shot down by the guns of the very place – the House – he'd been travelling to. He told them he was on a quest, and he was. *I* was the quest. He was on a quest to find me. This makes me sound of great importance, and I was. I am.

Because, you see, Jizania Tiger, in her youth, over a hundred years ago, had also left this City, and gone to live in the House. (No one says why. Honestly, I should just think she'd have preferred to.) I don't know how the House is related to this City. But obviously it was, then.

When she left, she promised, made a vow by the Law, to present to the Wolf Tower, when required, a girl of royal blood, from the House. A girl suitable to take on Ironel's duty, when Ironel gave it up.

If Jizania eventually forgot this vow, I don't know. Very likely. It was a damn silly nasty thing to have to remember.

But Nemian gave her the red flower, the Immortal, which was the token by which she'd know the time had come.

I suppose, as in certain stories I've read, maybe it was meant to be her own daughter, or granddaughter, she'd have to supply.

Did Jizania perhaps even tell Nemian that I was – that I *was* her granddaughter, her daughter's child?

You see, Jizania lied to Nemian, and she lied to me. And she knew and doubtless told him, he'd better lie to me too. Even when he started to have doubts I was the princess-girl Jizania had assured him I was. By then I was all he could get. I *did* come from the House. I have the House accent – which Ironel would recognize. Perhaps I'd do. And I was daft enough to believe him, to stay with him.

He did nearly lose me, that once, in Peshamba. But when he knew he might, he rushed to me and pleaded to try to get me back. He really was desperate and afraid that night. When he said his life wouldn't be worth anything without me, that *wasn't* a lie at all.

I said, the Law is the LAW. If he'd come back empty-handed, he'd have lost his title, his money, his wife. They'd have flung him in some cellar and left him there.

That's what the Law is like. You don't ever go against it.

Maybe he could just have run off in the wild, never come back. But he wanted to, was 'home-sick'. Or – well, he probably wanted Moon Silk.

That I'd be reluctant to come with him, was obvious. That is, if I'd known what they wanted me for. He wasn't surprised Jizania hadn't warned me, or told me everything. Or that he had to pretend.

That's all bad enough. But there's this other thing. Jizania was determined to send me off with Nemian, to keep her vow. So did she lie to me as well about my mother being royal? She couldn't say both my parents were royalty – I'd have seen the House wouldn't exile a prince and a princess. But the story of a princess falling in love with her servant rang true.

Of course, Ironel knew my name, or the full name Jizania told me was mine. Claidissa Star. Jizania must also have promised the Law she'd give this name to the chosen child. But then, you see, she could just have made sure some child of around the right age, any old child, *did* get this name. And that just happened to be me. So my name doesn't prove a thing.

And she'd seen I was nuts on Nemian. So I'd go on with the lie in any case, making him believe I was a princess and *worthy* of him.

I mean, do I strike you as princess material?

Heaven knows who I really am. Or who I really was—

Because now, I belong here, to the Tower. To the Law. To this place of stones, where their statues make even animals ugly.

And for this I gave up Argul. I made him think I didn't care. And that ring he dropped – oh, it was for me. Of course it was. He was for me, and I was for him. And anyway, even if he was just being kind – I could have been out there, in the world, in the Waste-which-isn't. Free. I could cry or laugh until I was sick. But instead, I'll go on writing. There's more to say. If you can stand it.

THE LAW: KEEPING

In the evening, I dined with Ironel.

Her apartment is sprawling. The size of the Travellers' Rest. Maybe not quite.

The Wolf Tower, as Nemian told me in non-lying mode, is the most powerful of the four Towers that rule the City on Wide River.

But the food wasn't up to much.

She only drinks her mud drink. I think it's because she hasn't got teeth, and doesn't dare chip the fabulous pearl ones.

Candles burned on an iron candlebranch that was standing on the table, and was taller than I am.

Why am I talking about candles?

By then, she'd shown me the holy part of the Tower. Holy used to mean to do with God, but now, despite Nemian's poetic spoutings that I liked so much, the Law the Wolf Tower makes is 'holy', and more holy than anything else.

The Law.

I don't know how to start to tell you. It's – it's – I'd better calm down. Again, I'll start again.

Once, all four Towers had a say in making the Law. Then there was a fight, or something, which the Wolf Tower won. So now the Wolf Tower does it, and everyone else obeys.

There are no servants, no maids. Only slaves. But the royal people who fill the City, and who the slaves serve, they too – are slaves. Slaves to the Law of the Wolf Tower. And so am I. I have been since I let Nemian escape from the House. Or even since I first thought I loved him.

It *stinks*.

The holy area, in which I now 'live', clusters around the main room, which they call the Room.

It isn't – amazingly – very big, this Room.

But it's black as dead burnt wood.

Huge lamps, too large for the Room, burn with pale, feverish fires.

Along the walls are shelves, and stacked there, like the books in the House library, are black boxes. And in the boxes, carefully filed and preserved by slaves of the Room, who suffer if they get it wrong, are cards with the names of every man, woman, child and infant in the City. There are even names of ones who've died – or, I hope, maybe run away. But they keep them anyway, with a red mark on the little card.

They enter new ones too. I saw this, the first night. *She* did it. Ironel.

The slaves brought a box, and another slave, from a house in the City that had had a baby, brought a card with the baby's name. Ironel took the card, read it, *smiled*, and put it on top of the box. That was all. The slave has to number and file it correctly. And, as I said, if he or she doesn't—

Bizarre enough.

But what actually catches one's attention in the Room at once, are the Dice.

Ironel said they were dice.

I said, (you see, my light's not put out yet) (don't know why not) 'What are Dice, madam?'

She told me, and told me their use in the Law. Do you know about dice? I'm still a bit blank really. The Dice have eight sides. Every side is painted with a number, from one to eight, inclusive.

How to show you. Well – let me draw it.
They are this shape:

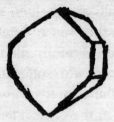

Like some cut diamonds – almost. There are only two of them.

They're held up in silver-gilded sort of – things. Which remind me of egg-cups, only with pieces cut out, so most of the shape of the Dice is visible.

And the dice can move. They have to. They spin and turn over in many directions. This happens four times a day, at dawn, at noon, at sunset, at midnight.

What makes them spin like this I don't understand. Some mechanism. But Ironel has to be there. And – once I've learnt – *I* have to be there. Instead of Ironel.

They call her the Wolf's Paw.

That's what I'll be called.

Wolf's Paw.

She *reads* the Dice when they come to rest, from the way in which all the numbered sides fall and face. And from that, looking in three books of ancient mathematics, which lie handy on a marble table in the Room, she can tell what the Law is saying must be done. And who must do it.

Although the Dice must often fall the same way – only two of them you see, and only eight sides each – apparently the day, and time of day always make a difference, or something to do with the maths – or what phase of the moon we're in – can you follow this? I can't.

So, I don't understand the books, or the Dice.

Or the way she can tell who must do what.

But apparently one *can* work it out, in numbers. Every spin of the Dice shows something someone has to do. You then tie up the message the Dice give with sixteen City people (for the two lots of eight different sides.) And that happens four times a day.

So that's – I can't even work *that* out.

I'm hopeless with numbers – four times sixteen – that's sixty-four people every day and night. (I worked it out on a different bit of paper.)

And whatever the Wolf's Paw tells them the Law says they must do, these sixty-four, they MUST. Each day.

Ironel gave me examples.

Nemian married Moon Silk because a fall of the Dice told him he should. (How about her?)

And Nemian came after me and found me, and brought me back here, because another fall of the Dice said he had to. (And how about *me*?)

The point is, if you're picked and you don't

obey, or you blow it, they imprison you under the City, in dank darkness, where the River seeps through. (She liked telling me about that, as well.)

Apart from mere horror, I can barely add up. Science is a mystery to me. How in the world's name am I going to master these awful Dice, these dreadful books of numbers and moon phases?

I didn't admit this. Just stood there, all cool.

Ironel let me see her make her judgement that sunset. It looked easy when she did it. But then she's done it for over fifty years. The Dice whirl and end up sideways or upright. She goes over and looks at them. Then she walks to the books. She makes a big thing about the books, keeps telling me there are only these three in the City, and how precious they are. (She showed me, in them, the hundreds of columns of numbers and my head went round like the Dice.)

She ran her finger down the columns, flipped pages, clicked her tongue on her pearls.

Then she spoke the Law, and the slaves wrote down each order. After this, messengers, (slaves) of the Wolf Tower, carry the orders to the lucky persons concerned.

The messages of the Law were frightful, though.

Some man (number 903, I think) had to leave his house and go and live on the street as 'best he could'. (Incredible.) And number 5,334, a little girl, was to be made to wear the disguise of a snail, complete with shell.

I forget the others. They weren't so bad. No, one was. I don't even want to write it.

But I will write it. I don't remember the number, or who. But they had to dive into the river, and swim up and down. They might rest on islands, or the banks, for a few minutes when 'exhausted'. Their relatives might bring them food and 'comforts'.

There was no indication when this punishment would end. If it ever would. It wasn't called a punishment.

And this – *this* – is the *Law*.

They live here, and some people can go their whole lives without ever the Dice summoning up their numbers and names, so they need never do anything but enjoy themselves. Or they might be told to do something rather stupid, but not unnice, like going and buying a new shirt.

Or they might be told they must have a baby, before a year has passed.

Or that they must stand naked on a wall. Or go into the desert and fight a lion.

And I'm going to have to find this out from the Dice. And I'm then going to have to tell them. I'm going to be Wolf's Paw. To be *her*.

She said, I'd grow old here.

If I don't learn, God knows what they'll do to me. And I won't be able to.

But I don't *want* to be able to. I don't want to hurt people, make fools of them, blight their lives like this, and smiling as I do it, as *she* does.

My rooms are large. There's a bathroom, a bed-room, and a living room. Brocades and furs and fireplaces and lamps.

One wall with dresses thick with gold and jewels. I hate them.

Five slaves to wait on me.

When I take her place, I'll have more. I'll have everything I 'want'.

Except I must always be available for when the Dice mechanically turn, to read the books and interpret the Law. And give it.

That night, after the midnight Dice, I made believe I'd gone to sleep in the luxurious white satin bed.

I got up in blind darkness, and tried to go out.

But the slaves were there, leaping up to 'serve' me.

And their eyes are like the eyes of the moon alligators in the marsh. Cold and blind. Without a mind or heart.

Sometimes the Wolf's Paw goes out in a pro-cession, she'd told me. Next day I asked to go walking.

No obstacle. Except the five slaves who walked with me. And that man in a white uniform, with the rifle.

Very few people passed us. Most were carried in chairs by slaves.

None of the slaves have faces. Well they do, but

they might as well be made of paper. They don't seem human.

The buildings soar into the never changing rainy gloom.

I prowl these rooms. The windows have cute lattices of gilded iron, and anyway are ten man-heights from the ground, or more. I'm a prisoner.

Well, I have considered various tricks – the sort you read of in books. Giving slaves the slip, running very fast, pretending to be ill in case they then relax their watchfulness, assuming they are watchful . . . which they are, aren't they? But somehow, I don't think this will work, any of it. I mean, they are always there. And the City itself does watch. Not crystals, like Peshamba, black poking things, like guns, turning to follow you on the streets.

Everyone's name is in those boxes, even mine, now, and hers.

I'm so afraid I don't even feel loss. And when she lectures me on the mathematics in the precious books, she seems to think I understand – and I *don't*, of course I don't. I was never educated. Two and two make three.

Is she mad? Or just so old – she asks questions and I attempt to answer, I bluff or I say nothing, and she doesn't fault me. She nods.

I haven't seen anyone else for some time. Only the slaves, and the guard in white. And occasionally people passing far below on the paved streets of this doomy City. And her.

The Law is a game. I mean, they play a *game*, and call it a law, and failure to obey it is death.

And Ironel is keeper of the Law until I learn the rules. And then I'm the keeper. (And when I think, the Rituals of the House used to annoy me.)

Nemian seems like someone I made up. Argul does too. And you – well, I *did* make you up. But oh, you, you, help me – tell me what to do – help, help me, you're the only one I can turn to. And obviously, you can't answer.

How curious. It was as if I heard you, calling. All sorts of words and voices. And it did help me.

Thank you . . .

Thank you.

WOLVES

She's ill.

She did the dawn Law today – I don't have to be there for those – then went back to bed.

A slave told me, and I had to go and visit her. Another slave handed me one of those red flowers to give her. Apparently that's a polite way to show her I think she'll soon get better.

(Would have liked to chuck it out of a window. Didn't.)

Ironel sat up in her bed, which is like a boat for size, with curtains of golden chains.

She looked all right to me.

When she'd sent everyone out, she said to me, 'I've never told you the reason for the Law, have I, which I must, since you're learning so fast and so very well.'

I gulped. She's dotty.

But she said, 'Random blows, and insane adventures. The Law copies life.'

That was all. I didn't understand, but just nodded, coolly, and gazed into space as if deeply thinking.

Then she made me really jump. She *laughed*. It was an awful old cackle, you can imagine, and those pearl teeth bouncing about in it.

'Claidissa, dear,' she said, when she could, 'you may have to take over the Law very soon. I'm ill. It's too much for me. So be ready. Get fit. Go out for a walk, Claidissa. Walk around our spectacular City. Look at the darling River. Have some exercise. *Think* about what I've told you. You will be a Wolf of the Tower. And those powerful Dice, those delicious rare books, those important boxes, by which we live.'

I was shaking. I said, 'Yes, madam.'

Her word is Law, isn't it. I'd have to take over. And I'd have to have a walk! (And go down the Tower again in one of those lifters.)

So I'll do that. I'll walk. I can do that. I *can't* read the books or do the Law thing. I might as well jump in the River.

I don't think I said, I had to wear the proper clothes now always. People were supposed to know who I was – the next WP. No wonder no one spoke to me, or looked.

These dresses are so heavy. I felt like a beetle or a lizard, all wrapped up in scales and bits of carapace. My hair too, wound up on a golden comb, and pulling. I didn't know myself in mirrors any more. Which fitted with how I felt, pretty much.

This time, though, down in the City, I studied things with more care. I'm not sure why. Guilt maybe, because I wasn't going to jump in the River.

The people who passed, carried in ornate chairs, or sometimes walking, with slaves pattering behind, they all looked the same. They looked like me. Overdressed, starched, and so unhappy.

Well I didn't need to be a genius, did I, to realize why. They lived here because they felt they had to, or surely they'd have gone. And while they did, even if the Law so far had *never* fallen on them or anyone they cared about, four times every day they knew it still *could*, and probably would.

I wandered down below the Wolf Tower, and along the banks, quays, they say here, where tall grim ships are tied by chains. Then the River gets wide again, and you can't see the far bank, which is just how Nemian described it.

Rain plished miserably.

And I noticed someone swimming in that icy grey water.

I knew who it was. Who it had to be. The one whose number I don't remember.

Tears flooded down my face. I clenched my fists.

This was all crazy. It was a nightmare.

One of the slaves came over and offered me a hanky to mop up. The one with the umbrella I'd sent off crept close again.

I turned on them.

'I want to be left alone.' Their faces were flat, and told me nothing. 'All right. Stand there. I'm just going across into that square. I'm going – to buy something. Don't follow. I don't need you yet.'

To my amazement, as I started to walk they didn't. Even the guard with the rifle.

Was it so simple?

I'd never thought of this. That they'd just do what I said. Could I dodge away and make a run for it?

Where though? Beyond the City, I'd seen, was only that grey bare deserty land. And anyway, would they let me go, that is, the City itself? The House hadn't bothered to pursue me. I knew now why. Jizania had made sure Nemian and I got away. But here it would be different, although for the same reason.

I crossed the street and went into the square. Perhaps I should still try to make some plan—

215

There was a group of people over at the end of the square. That surprised me. I hadn't often seen any big group here before.

They do use money in the City. I'd been given a chest full of those blue-green notes Nemian had had. Although everyone seemed to be royal, some of the people here made things, although they weren't very good. They sold them to each other. (Clothes and food and urgent stuff the slaves saw to, without of course being paid.)

Was someone here selling something? The crowd seemed very interested, which wasn't usual either.

There seemed to be someone sitting on the ground. And two others lounging against a pillar. The ground here wasn't made for sitting on, and the pillars weren't for lounging against. It also looked as if these three odd people were slaves, too, because they weren't sparkling.

As I got nearer and nearer, I saw there were children as well, standing staring in their awful tight jewellery-beetle clothes. But suddenly they all squealed, and there was a brilliant flash, yellow, blue, and up into the air shot all these burning stars—

Fireworks! I knew at once from what Nemian had said. The City had fireworks, but I'd never seen any before.

There were slaves standing around the back of the crowd, also watching the man sitting on the ground.

Then there was a little *crack*, and the children went *Ooooh*! like *real* children. And into the air rose a bird of fire. It was emerald and purple, and slowly, beautifully, it spread a fan-tail of gold—

A peacock. A firework peacock.

I'd reached the edge of the crowd. No. The three men, now I could really see them, didn't belong in this City. They were old and *filthy*, their long old hair and long scraggly old beards full of bits of mud and twig, like badly made nests. Their faces looked like crumpled dirty rags. Their clothes *were* rags. Layers of rags and gruesome old fur jackets.

The seated old man moved his hands, in dirty darned gloves, and out of the thin air between them bloomed a ball of colours. And birds flew out of it, white, like pigeons. They flew up, and I thought *Oh God, what will happen to them here*? Because I hadn't seen a single bird or animal in the City that wasn't stone. Not even a fly. And never trees, or any flowers – only those red things called Immortals.

However, the birds dissolved in light. They hadn't been real.

And of course, then I thought of how Argul had taken the living sparrow out of Teil's ear.

But I wasn't going to cry any more.

The children were laughing and pointing. Little rabbits made of light were jumping round their ankles. (Had they ever seen rabbits?) And there

217

were some smiles from the adults, too. Even – my God – one of the slaves was smiling. Hey!

The darker old man leaning on the pillar was giving me a funny look. The other one abruptly shouted three very strong words.

The crowd didn't take much notice. They didn't know these words weren't polite, as I hadn't when I used to hear them first.

'Tronking okk grulps!'

Oddly, the second darker old man turned and thumped, with surprising force, the other old man on the chest.

And the other old man roared in a hurt voice: 'Watch it, Mehm. She's h—'

'Then don't make a scene, man.'

I wasn't standing on the street any more. I was floating up and up. Like the magical chemical lights Argul's scientist-magician mother must have taught him how to make.

He was getting to his feet now, the doddery seated old man. Of the three, he could have won a prize for the disgustingness of his beard. He took some time, too, so stiff and ungainly.

The children were clamouring for more tricks. Instead he was handing each of them an apple baked in toffee, from Peshamba, probably. And to each adult – and slave – a Peshamban chocolate sweet in coloured paper.

Then he came grunting and hobbling over, snuffling, leering, his ghastly mucky beard flapping, until he stood in front of me, and I had to look up to reach his eyes.

Behind him, Mehmed and Ro slapped each other (clouds of filth rose) and guffawed. The children were prancing and tearing chunks out of the toffee apples. The adults were wonderingly unwrapping their sweets. It broke your heart. You could see they too had never been given anything very nice, and *never* for free.

'Hallo, Claidi-sheepy-baa,' said Argul, through his brilliant disguise, the cakes of make-up and mud and horsehair stuck on his face. 'Got yourself in a mess again, I gather.'

'Yes, Argul.'

'Don't cry. I never saw you cry.'

'It's the rain.'

'Oh yeah. Of course.'

In the porch of a building, out of the rain, we spoke so quickly to each other, as if there was no time. But as the Peshamban CLOCK said, There's time enough for everything.

(Through the rain, I could see my slaves and guard, still unmoving at the edge of the square, waiting, presumably noticing me talking to this wild old man, and not knowing what went on.)

'Why did you follow me? You were so angry—'

'That changed. And I didn't trust *him*. So. It took a while to get here. He'd talked a lot about his perfect City and glorious Wolf Tower. Can't miss it, can you. What an eyesore. Wolves aren't like that.'

'No . . . What are they like?'

He laughed. 'Still Claidi. They're brave and loyal. They fight when they have to, or they don't fight. They like each other and stick together. Hulta. That's wolves.'

'Argul—'

'I saw you ditched your guard. If we just walk slowly, maybe—'

'No, I've thought about all that. They won't let me go. If I got away, they'd come after. It's their rotten Law.'

'We have to take the chance. I've brought Sirree. Yes, she's well. She missed you.'

'I missed her. Oh, Sirree—'

I stood gazing at this dirty wreck who was HIM.

In the holes and tatters of his shirt, I saw the glass charm winking.

'I can't, Argul. It's too dangerous.'

'Chicken.'

'I am. And for you, too. I don't want you to get hurt.'

He put his hand up over the charm. 'See this,' he said.

'Yes, I remember.'

'Remember I looked at it when you were in the Sheeper chariot?'

'Yes.'

'It tells me things. My mother – she said if ever I saw – if I saw a woman who meant something to me—' He stopped.

He was embarrassed. Here, in the middle of all this. I looked down, to give him a chance. And he said, 'The stuff in the bulb, that you think looks like glass, is a chemical. It reacts if *I* do. I mean, if the feeling is real. And it does react, Claidi.' He slipped the charm-which-wasn't off, and held it in his hand, and I saw the glass-which-wasn't turn cloudy, and then a kind of movement happened inside. That was all. But it was love I was looking at.

I thought how Mehmed had whooped when he leaned over and saw it too, and threw a knife and caught it in his teeth.

'Argul, I daren't go with you. I mean, I *do* want to—'

'You've said this before. Look what happened.'

'Do you *know*,' I asked him, 'about the *Law*?'

'Yes. We're foreigners, they can have a moan to us. I know all of it and it's—' he said a word I hadn't ever heard before.

'Well,' I faltered, 'then you see—'

'Claidi,' said Argul. 'Do you really believe two dice rolling about and some old books of rubbish can tell a whole city to live like this, in terror? You saw those kids over there. And the rest of them. Dice aren't wicked. Books aren't. People can be. *People* caused this.'

Something clicked in my mind. I can't describe it any other way. I stood speechless.

'Claidi—'

'Wait – just a moment – oh—'

And he did wait. He likes me, too. He thinks I have a right to scrabble around, trying to think for myself.

Then I spoke to him *very* fast. He listened.

When I'd finished, he said, 'Claidi, I wish you were a fool. It'd be easier.'

The kids were playing games on the grey square despite the rain. Running about and screaming with joy. The adults, mouths full of chocolate, didn't stop them.

Oh, I can see now why Nemian went mad and played about so much, when he got out of this place.

I feel sorry for Nemian. And his exquisite moon-wife.

Mehmed and Ro were standing near in the rain, wet and nosy.

'All right,' Argul said to me. 'Try. But if not—'

I shook my head.

Then he caught me and kissed me. Through that *beard*. And even so – (They jeered, whistled, called out 'Hultai chura!' Which means Leader's sweetheart. That was far away. They fell silent, tired.)

I'm writing this now in such a hurry. I saw love in the 'glass' 'charm'. You could miss it so easily. Yet it's so vast. It's miraculous. Just like

222

how I found him, walking into that square, as if I had to.

And even if I fail tonight, if I die, I'll have that kiss to keep.

It isn't like being scalded. It's like having wings.

FIREWORKS

When I met Ironel in the Room, at midday, she looked me over, and immediately said, 'I don't remember that ring.'

'My mother, Twilight Star, left it for me. Princess Jizania passed it on.'

'Is it a diamond? What a barbaric setting. But. I like it. It's like – a star. How fitting.'

'Thank you.'

'She must have loved you,' said Ironel, regretfully.

I don't know if she did, or even if she was called Twilight. Argul gave me the ring, which the Peshambans returned to him. And he *does* love me. And I know. (And the ring belonged to *his* mother, so it's almost not a lie.)

I watched very carefully as Ironel did the noon reading and spoke more awful Law I'm not even going to put down.

Leaving for that walk, I'd been praying Ironel would continue doing this for a long time. Now, as the business ended, I said, 'Madam, you should go back to bed. You look so ill.'

She didn't. She looked repulsively healthy in her iron-old way.

And she narrowed her eyes at me.

'Do I, Claidissa? Indeed.'

'As you say, madam, you've trained me for this. It's my job now. I'll take over.'

Remember how I described the alligators? Those great long mouths of teeth? Well, that was how she smiled. Her mouth seemed to undo her face in two pieces. And her poisonous eyes were bright.

'Ah, Claidissa. That would be kind. Two or three days in my bed, that should set me up again. And yes, you're so wise now in the reading of the Law. After all. Perhaps I needn't return.'

I hadn't been sure. I mean, it was only about an hour ago I'd really thought of it. And, even if I was right, this might still be some plan of hers to hurt me. It was a chance I was going to take.

The same as when I shouted at the 'bandits' I'd bite off a nose before I'd give in. I *won't* be stopped. Not any more.

I bowed low to her.

'I think, lady, I'll just stay here in the holy Room. Make myself more familiar with the wonderful books and things.'

'Do, Claidissa.' Then she did up her face again. She said, her voice suddenly hollow and ancient, 'I've waited so many years for this hour.'

And she turned and stalked out, her cane rapping like shots on the floor.

One huge wave of panic.

I ignored it. Sometimes it's all you can do.

'This Room is freezing,' I yacked to the nearest slave. The Room wasn't. If anything, it got too hot from the lamps. 'Fetch me two or three lighted braziers.'

After I had the braziers in, burning away roastingly, I sent the slaves out. I had about seven hours until sunset. And if I was truly successful about this, some extra hours until midnight.

Would she suddenly come back, 'Oh I'm so much better!'? Somehow I really didn't think so. She'd had enough of this, after fifty years. And that means she must have had enough of herself too.

Because if I was right – *If* I was—

She'd kept telling me I'd mastered the Law. Well, now I *would*.

At the House, I'd been used to hard work. And this was. Climbing up the moveable step-ladder, getting down all the top boxes, then the lower ones, kneeling to get the lowest. Making sure I put them all back exactly as I'd found them. Well. Not quite.

Once or twice I went out into the room outside the Room. Mostly to cool down. There was a window, and I was faintly surprised, because the grey

225

day changed. The clouds went blowing off slowly down the River. The sky turned palest blue.

That was good. I could check on sunset better.

No slaves loitered. Outside, the corridor leading to Ironel's apartment was empty – almost. I could just see my white guard's rifle propped up there, as he waited with my slaves.

The Room was scorching. It was like being in an oven. But I went on with my work.

When I walked into the outer room later, and the western window was starting to flush, and the sun was actually there, gleaming low on to the River, I had the sense to stop.

I just stood in the Room then, haughty and poised, and waited for the slaves of the Law to appear.

They did, dead on time. They couldn't ever risk being late.

I could already hear noises in the egg-cup things that held the dice. They were warming up to spin.

Partly, I'd had a last fear she might come back simply to watch me. She hadn't. If she had, that might have meant I'd been wrong. Or maybe not. I'll never know about Ironel, or Jizania, come to that. Maybe they felt they couldn't change, but knew that, in choosing me, they'd selected someone who wouldn't put up with it, and that I'd do what I have.

I hope they thought that. For their sakes.

The slaves filed in, and we all stood religiously in proper awe.

And the Dice chugged and spun. And stopped. Now was the moment.

I walked over and examined the Dice with care. Then I hesitated in thought. Then I went to the three old books. I rustled about in them, peering, shaking my head. I frowned. Pompously I spoke.

The slaves wrote everything down.

There was one difference. *I* gave them the numbers *and* the names, so they didn't have to look them up in the boxes. I'd chosen these numbers and names earlier. The slaves didn't argue.

Now I can't even recall all the things I said. Or can I? Claidi's Law . . .

One man had to go and buy all the badly made pots some woman had been making, and tell her they were fantastic. And another man had to go and light all the candles in his house, and then ask all his friends to dinner. And then they had to ask him back.

I told a woman she must fall in love, I remember that. And six separate families I told to dress their children in loose clothes, and then play with them.

I told two men to leave the City and buy plants, and some animals, and bring them back and let people see and look after them. And another couple to get organized a way of making gardens and orchards.

Two or three were ordered to find something really funny and laugh at it.

Not that brilliant, I admit. But the Law that sunset was no more stupid than it had been before. And it might not do so much harm.

No one challenged me. The slaves went sloping off with the orders, and when they were gone, I shut the door of the Room, again, and finished my work.

Seems to me, I'll often dream about it. Carrying all those black boxes to the braziers and tipping in all the cards with names and numbers, and watching them burn so brightly, and then vanish for ever.

Or maybe I'll dream more about all the pages I tore, every single one, from the precious books, the only ones in the City – as Ironel had kept on telling me. Page after page of tough parchment, which sometimes burned with a weird brown flame.

Sparks flew up to the ceiling, like Argul's magic, or the Peshambans' CLOCK.

My arms and back ached. My throat was sore and my eyes smarting from smoke.

I was hungry too. Although not very.

Finally, it was finished. And then I did the very last thing.

I took a burning wick in its holder out of one of the lamps, and carried it over to the Dice. And carefully and thoroughly, I burned off every number painted on them. Until each of the sixteen sides was just a smudge. They could spin all they liked. It wouldn't mean a thing.

Then I burned a message in the black wall, burned it so it went white, and was easy to see and hard to get rid of.

It said:

This is the Law of the Wolf Tower: There is to be no MORE Law.

Under which I wrote my name: *Claidissa Star.*

Then I thought, WHAT HAVE I DONE???

But it was too late. So I picked up my gold bag with this book in it, and ten ink pencils and pen-things I'd stolen from the Tower, left the Room, and the other room, and walked down the corridor. My slaves were at the end as always, and the guard in white with the rifle. I had the feeling they'd all been asleep.

It was full night. The windows were black. But I could see stars over the City.

I knew the way to the nearest lifter. The slaves and guard padded with me. Actually, there were seven slaves now. Increased, no doubt, because I'd read the Dice.

'I think I'll take a quick walk, before the midnight Law,' I chattily told them. So we all piled in the lifter and down we jumbled to the ground floor.

When we got to the quite small door by which I usually went out, some odd sounds were ringing over the City.

The slaves didn't do anything, but the guard took firm hold of his rifle.

'It's all right,' I said to him. 'It's only music. And someone singing.'

Had I told someone to sing? Probably.

Elsewhere – barking – dogs? I'd never known there were dogs here. And then laughter, quite a lot of it.

Many windows seemed alight. Or brighter, warmer. Something.

I said loudly to the seven slaves, 'You stay there, please. Sit down. You should relax.' And they sat in a row on a bench by the door. Then I said to the guard, 'I've always so admired that rifle. May I look at it?' And the fool gawped at me, and then handed the rifle to me. I was WP, wasn't I. I could have what I wanted.

The rifle wasn't with me for long, though. I turned and gave it to Argul, who was now standing there just beyond the doorway, as arranged.

'You took your time, Claidibaabaa.'

'I warned you. It took ages.'

'You're ready now?'

'Yes.'

Argul's disguise was gone. He looked – there wasn't time to look.

Argul pushed the guard quite gently back into the Wolf Tower. The guard seemed convinced he'd wake up in a minute.

Until Argul shut the door on him.

Ro and Mehmed were already dragging me on to a horse – difficult in the armoured City dress – but I made it. (And the dress split.) 'Sirree?' I whispered, 'Sirree, you *are* Sirreee—' And Sirree blew down her velvet nose at me.

Then Argul was also up on his horse, and we were riding, so fast, like the night itself, all made of black horses, racing.

I looked back once. The Tower door was still shut. Nothing seemed to be happening there.

And as we galloped, I glimpsed those gun-things that watched, swivelling after us – and I cowered each time – but nothing happened there either.

The City people had forgotten how to think. They'd have to remember. I hoped the slaves would remember, too.

I tried to call to Argul as we raced neck and neck, through echoing caverns of stone, the hoofs of the horses sounding like hammers.

'There's still a chance – if I misjudged her – Ironel – a chance she might just go on as she did before—'

'Can't hear you, Claidi,' Argul shouted back.

So I had to answer myself. Yes, there was a chance Ironel might do that. If I'd guessed correctly, she hadn't used the books or read the Dice for years. She'd said any old number she thought of, and as for the Law, she'd just been making it up. And what she'd made up was pretty evil. (Except for Nemian and herself. Letting him marry someone he must really have wanted, and sending him on a quest to fetch what Ironel wanted – me.)

She was old and mad. But then again, she knew – I'd swear she did – what I was going to do. She left me no choice. Scaring me, making me angry. Leaving me on my own in the Room. I mean, she practically told me how to do it.

Even so, I longed for some sign I'd done the right thing.

We got out of the City much more quickly than I'd have thought possible. Perhaps it's not so huge as I believed. It had only seemed too big for me.

The starlit land rolled away, away to other places. Away to the Hulta camp, and Blurn and Teil and Dagger, where they were, far along the River, which was only a river. Away to somewhere where I could keep still, and breathe and be. And where I can stop bothering you, my invented friend, who's stuck by me and helped so much.

The starlit land. The Waste that isn't.

We paused, in some thin trees on a rise, to give the horses a rest. (Sirree was terrific.)

I kept saying to myself, Did I do the right thing? (I keep saying that, still. What do you think?) But you see, I couldn't stay, if I had a chance of escape. And I couldn't leave them as they were. *I'm trouble*, as Argul said. (And as Nemian never knew.) And by then, on that rise, it was well past midnight, the time of the Law.

Argul took my hand, and shook it up and down. His armlets jangled, and for some reason we both grinned.

'Ring not too painful?' he asked.

I said, truthfully, 'It feels like it's part of my hand.'

And just then, dull thunder, a roar. I nearly screamed.

'Oh God. Argul – *Argul* – the city – it's exploded – it's on fire!'

We stared. And above, the night changed colour. Silver, scarlet, amber, violet, gold and white.

It was Mehmed who said, explaining, pleased, 'No, Claidi. It must be a celebration. They're letting off about two thousand fireworks.'

DAUGHTER OF STORMS

Louise Cooper

Born in a supernatural storm, under a crimson sun, Shar is destined for the Sisterhood.

Innocent of the power she controls, Shar is of great value to others – who patiently lie waiting for such a soul.

But as Shar begins to realise her gift, the terror begins . . .

In a land where the gods of Order and Chaos rule – a deadly power is rising. Can Shar summon the elements to become the Dark Caller?

'Daughter of Storms has everything, including a narrative that makes the book hard to put down.' Diana Wynne Jones *THE TELEGRAPH*

THE DARK CALLER

Louise Cooper

The chilling sequel to *Daughter of Storms*.

Shar, the Dark Caller, has a unique power – to harness good spirits, and to destroy anyone who threatens her. Now someone wants revenge . . .

Lured into a web of terror and deceit, can Shar defy the forces that threaten her once again? And will the gods be on her side this time?

KEEPERS OF LIGHT

Louise Cooper

The third gripping volume in the
Daughter of Storms trilogy . . .

With her unique powers, Shar is driven
to unlock the secrets of The Maze – a
magical gateway through time.

The Maze gives Shar the power to right
an old wrong, but also to change the
course of history.

But as she faces its many terrifying
dimensions – will The Maze lead Shar
into deadly temptation?

POWER TO BURN

Anna Fienberg

Dark family secrets . . .

Revenge for a lost love . . .

The power of magic . . .

Roberto arrives in Italy to visit his family and slowly uncovers the tragic story that lies buried at its heart.

Angelica knows the magic power is stirring. Now they can both feel it burning in their fingertips. Lucrezia is ready to take her revenge.

But can fire and forgiveness melt anger cold as ice?

Can they stop her before she destroys them all?

SWORD AND SORCERY

Alan Brown

'*Alan Brown is a masterly storyteller*'
Elizabeth Laird

A drowned world where forest covers the islands that remain. While people struggle to survive, other species grow to giant size. Mythical beasts stalk the land and sorcery is rife.

Only Art can save his family destruction and build a future in this strange land. Only he can lead the treacherous quest to defeat the fearsome Dragonfolk.

But does he have the strength and the power to defeat the sorcery in their midst?

Will sword or sorcery triumph?